THE STENCH OF DEATH

"This was no ordinary rubout," Windy said to Matt. They walked their horses toward the grisly tableau that lay before them. It was all real—the blood, the torn bodies, the smoldering wagons, the relentless stench . . .

The scout knelt down beside the body of a woman. Before Matt could say anything, Windy pried the woman's jaws apart. Reaching inside he withdrew something.

"What have you got?" Matt asked.

"This." Windy opened his hand. In his palm was a button from a United States Army uniform . . .

EASY COMPANY

EASY COMPANY

AND THE DOG SOLDIERS

JOHN WESLEY HOWARD

A JOVE BOOK

EASY COMPANY AND THE DOG SOLDIERS

A Jove Book / published by arrangement with
the author

PRINTING HISTORY
Jove edition / April 1983

ISBN: 0-515-06359-2

Jove books are published by Jove Publications, Inc.,
200 Madison Avenue, New York, N.Y. 10016. The words
"A JOVE BOOK" and the "J" with sunburst are trademarks
belonging to Jove Publications, Inc.

PRINTED IN THE UNITED STATES OF AMERICA

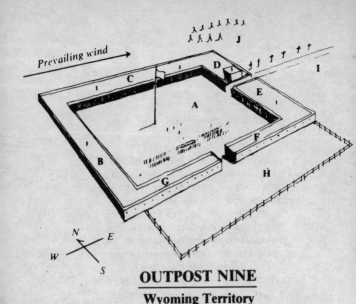

OUTPOST NINE
Wyoming Territory
KEY

A. Parade and flagstaff

B. Officers' quarters ("officers' country")

C. Enlisted men's quarters: barracks, day room, and mess

D. Kitchen, quartermaster supplies, ordnance shop, guardhouse

E. Suttler's store and other shops, tack room, and smithy

F. Stables

G. Quarters for dependents and guests; communal kitchen

H. Paddock

I. Road and telegraph line to regimental headquarters

J. Indian camp occupied by transient "friendlies"

INTERIOR   OUTSIDE

OUTPOST NUMBER NINE
(DETAIL)

Outpost Number Nine is a typical High Plains military outpost of the days following the Battle of the Little Big Horn, and is the home of Easy Company. It is not a "fort"; an official fort is the headquarters of a regiment. However, it resembles a fort in its construction.

The birdseye view shows the general layout and orientation of Outpost Number Nine; features are explained in the Key.

The detail shows a cross-section through the outpost's double walls, which ingeniously combine the functions of fortification and shelter.

The walls are constructed of sod, dug from the prairie on which Outpost Number Nine stands, and are sturdy enough to withstand an assault by anything less than artillery. The roof is of log beams covered by planking, tarpaper, and a top layer of sod. It also provides a parapet from which the outpost's defenders can fire down on an attacking force.

one ━━━━━━━━━━━━

    Dawn broke gently over the tawny plain. It didn't make a sound as it penetrated the retreating night; and all at once the day was there. Now the quick morning light fell across the tents of Tipi Town, the friendlies' village lying just to the northeast of the soldier outpost. A dog barked, while the pungent smell of burning buffalo chips, carried by the smoke of the cookfires, reached into the fresh, still-wet air. It had rained during the night.

    The new sun was well above the horizon now, its light glistening in the drops of water beading the grass stems of the rolling prairie. A blue jay called, and a small flock of chickadees flew low over the Indian pony herd, cropping the short buffalo grass. A grazing bell tinkled in the thin air. The sunlight, brighter now, washed the sod walls of Outpost Number Nine, the home of Easy Company, a mounted infantry detachment guarding the Wyoming Territory between the Bighorns and South Pass.

On the east wall by the lookout tower and gate, Private Al Gatwin—formerly Langley Albert Wingate, Jr.—looked out toward the deadline, across the area around the outpost that had been cleared of brush so that any approach could be seen immediately.

Private Gatwin, who had run away from his home back East to join the Army of the West, had been walking his post in a somber, lonely mood; but now, as the fresh sunlight touched his hands, his face, he suddenly felt the urge to sing.

He had the good sense to refrain, having been thoroughly instructed in army discipline by his squad leader, his platoon sergeant, and by the enlisted men's Ultimate Authority—First Sergeant Ben Cohen.

Private Gatwin was an impressionable youth, and intelligent; he was the quiet type, reliable, a good worker. At the same time, he was cautious as a consequence of having lied about his age and background in order to enlist. He carried just enough fear in him to breed a first-class soldier. Right now his wealthy Bostonian parents would have had difficulty in recognizing Langley Albert Wingate, Jr. as Private Al Gatwin.

For some unaccountable reason, Gatwin's thoughts had been occupied with a girl he had once seen—not even met, because of his impossible shyness—back in Boston, a girl with dancing blue eyes and a laughing mouth. But now, all at once, a call from the picket guard brought his attention to the perimeter line, where something was moving.

Behind him, across the parade, the door of the bachelor officers' quarters opened and First Lieutenant Matt Kincaid, Easy Company's adjutant and second-in-command, stepped out into the drying day. He stood for a moment, watching a lone eagle sweep down the long blue sky. From the stables came the brisk whinny of a horse, followed by a second animal's loud nicker.

Kincaid was a broad-shouldered man in his thirties, with narrow hips and a slightly sandy cast to his clean-cut features; he was tall, handsome, and—immediately obvious—resolute, yet there was humor behind his gray eyes. At this moment he had the sudden desire to scratch his right buttock, but Private Gatwin's call came down from the parapet.

"Wagon coming in. Civilian, and no escort."

Matt Kincaid reached instead to the side of his jaw and ran his forefinger along the bone, thinking how he would enjoy a mug of hot coffee. Then he turned on his heel and walked quickly toward the orderly room, deciding to send Four Eyes Bradshaw, the company clerk, for his coffee.

Meanwhile the wagon, drawn by a single swaybacked, spavined mule, had almost reached the gate. A huge man sat hunched forward in the driver's seat, his large elbows on his knees, his big-knuckled hands loosely holding the reins. He was dressed completely in black. Private Gatwin, looking down from the wall, wondered if maybe he was a preacher. Suddenly the man's dusty black wide-brimmed hat swung back and Gatwin was looking into the deepest-set eyes he had ever seen—eyes that at the same time seemed to glow.

Al Gatwin felt something like fear trickle through him. He had never seen such eyes; they were like hot coals in a couple of buggy-whip sockets, he thought, being gifted with a sometimes colorfully descriptive turn of mind. He tore his own eyes away as below him the gate swung open to admit the visitor. As the wagon passed into the parade, Gatwin now saw two passengers looking out from the tarpaulin behind the driver: a young, raven-haired girl with her mouth open, and a very young boy wearing a cap with an enormous bill over a stack of corn-yellow hair. He was biting the knuckle of his thumb.

● ● ●

Behind his desk, looking into those deep-set, burning eyes, Captain Warner Conway felt something he couldn't quite put a name to. The big, gaunt, beak-faced man stood bent over the other side of the desk, his great bony hands hanging a long way below the frayed cuffs of his black broadcloth coat.

Ethan Deal still wore his hat; his long, guttered face, sparsely covered with beard—though his eyebrows were fiercely bushy—canting down toward the commanding officer of Easy Company.

Seated across the room, near the young girl and the still younger boy, Matt Kincaid also felt the strangeness of the visitor; he was reminded of his own New England background with its stark winters and long, bleak silences.

"Won't you have a seat, Mr. Deal?" Conway said for the second time since the travelers had entered his office.

Ethan Deal again ignored the captain's offer, and said, "Captain Conway, I want you to do something about them Injuns and my mule Jessie."

Conway cast a glance at Kincaid, then returned his gaze to Ethan Deal, who had thus far avoided any answer to questions about himself, his family, or his destination. He had said only that he was from Massachusetts and had been looking for land to farm. Conway was at a loss to figure out how he had made it this far from home with his wagon and mule and two children.

"Mr. Deal," Matt said suddenly from across the room, "I'd like to get some details clear before we send out a patrol to investigate what happened. I believe you said that the band of Indians started out friendly."

"That is the size of it, sir." Deal straightened somewhat, facing Kincaid, though he was still bent over. Pushing back the wings of his coat, he slid the palms of his big, saddle-colored hands under his faded yellow galluses. Even out in this country, Matt thought, he was a striking figure, with his great height and his long face, its fixed, pewter-like eyes hard on his demand for justice and reprisal.

Now, suddenly, Deal removed his hat and sat down in the chair that Conway had twice offered.

"Like I already said to the captain, Lieutenant, them red devils braced us about three hours north of here, by a creek—don't know the name, but there was willows, a couple of high mounds. All gussied up they was, about a half-dozen. Scared the three of us." He sniffed. A drop of perspiration had formed on the end of his nose, but he didn't wipe it off. Conway waited, fascinated, for it to fall. A tough Yankee with two kids, he was thinking, the girl maybe eighteen or twenty at most, the boy probably ten; and all alone out here on the frontier. Yet Conway felt that Ethan Deal was somehow a good bit more than just a tough Yankee horsetrader. There was power in him, and at the same time something mysterious, as though a lot of him were living somewhere else at the same time he was standing here.

"Did they speak English?" Matt asked.

"They like to spoke it, and that surprised me; only they sort of had it all mixed up. Thought for a minute they'd been imbibing the devil's water." Deal paused, his tongue feeling swiftly around in his mouth for some particle of food or maybe tobacco that was bothering him.

"Anyhow," he continued after he'd found the offending foreign body and removed it, "the long and short of it was I finally figgered they was wanting to trade. Wanted to know had I anything to swap 'em. Well, I don't mind sayin' I been in the business since I was knee-high to a churchmouse. So I figgered I'd maybe offer them Jessie, my other mule. Jessie wasn't really pulling too good."

"What did they offer you?" Conway asked.

"I told 'em I wanted a horse. So they finally agreed

and rode off to their camp for one." He shook his head. "Them red marauders didn't appear to know much about mules. Still, Jessie was serviceable; yup, serviceable I'd allow."

Suddenly his face darkened. "Gol-dangit! Why you keep asking me these fool questions? I told you already what happened!"

"Mr. Deal," Conway said, leaning his forearms onto his desk. "Be patient. We are planning to send a patrol out to investigate. Now the Indians are sometimes pretty touchy, and we want to be sure of all our facts so we don't have any trouble flaring up."

Matt caught the special softening of Conway's Virginia accent, and he knew the captain was being extra patient.

Deal sniffed. Conway watched the drop of water that was still on the end of his nose.

"Did you find out what tribe they were?" Kincaid asked.

"Dunno. I ain't versed in such. All redskins is the same to me."

"How were they dressed? Did they have paint, feathers? What kind of weapons? Did they have guns?"

"They had bows an' arrers. A couple had spears. I didn't see no guns. 'Course they could've been hidden."

"So they rode off to get the horse," said Kincaid. "But then they didn't bring it back."

"What happened then?" Conway asked. "I know you already told us, Mr. Deal," he added swiftly, "but maybe you forgot a detail that would help identify the tribe. See, it would help us a great deal if we knew what tribe the Indians were."

Deal's nod seemed to be an acceptance of that. "I'd about gave up on 'em coming back with the hoss," he said, "but they did come, like I said. Only they went to steal Jessie. They didn't have no hoss at all." He glared

6

at Conway. "Captain, while we are sitting here jawing, them red devils is getting away."

"Please, Mr. Deal," Matt said, leaning forward with his elbows on his knees. "Just go over the shooting once again."

Deal's face darkened. "Like I said about a hundred times already, when they come back they didn't have no hoss, and there they was, unhitching Jessie. And my other mule, Hannah, to boot!"

"Stealing them?"

"They sure wasn't feeding 'em licorice sticks! Jessie and Hannah let out a couple brays would've woke the whole entire state of Massachusetts!"

"And then?" Conway asked. "They didn't have guns. Did they shoot some arrows?"

Deal looked quickly at the girl and boy, who, all through the conversation, had remained silent. Then he said, "I seed there was more of 'em when they come back, and I did feel myself getting nervous. On account of them two," he added quickly. "So I fired at 'em to scare 'em off. Wasn't tryin' to hit anyone." He paused. "'Course, by now it was dark. Fact is, if I'd have had my Henry which I lost back in Nebraska instead of this old muzzle-loader, I could've knocked a eyelash off a running rabbit, but it being dark like I said, I hit one of them Injuns; heard him yell. But then I hit poor Jessie." He sniffed. "It being dark, I wasn't about to get into fighting them red savages. Had my share coming through Nebraska, by God. The Lord be thanked I be here talking to you!"

Deal leaned forward again, this time slapping his big hand on his bony knee. "Captain, they made that trade, and we'd agreed on it."

"Sight unseen?"

"Sight unseen. That was the trade. I didn't see their hoss, but I made the agreement it had to be one could

7

pull my wagon. They agreed, by golly! And now it's on their account Jessie is dead. They owe me that horse, and I want it! And I want protection for us here!"

Unexpectedly, Conway turned to the girl and boy. "You haven't said anything, either of you," he said kindly. "But perhaps you might have noticed something special about the Indians, something that would help us tell what tribe they were."

The girl, who could have been eighteen, but might have been twenty, said, "They acted funny." There was no expression on her face.

"How, funny?" Matt asked.

She shrugged, and when she answered she didn't look at him, but kept her eyes on the carpet. "Two of them was riding their horses backwards, and they spoke funny. And they was laughing and like funning. I thought they was tipsy."

"Drunk?"

The girl nodded.

"Anything else?"

She shook her head, and then looked down at her hands lying in her lap. She was wearing a faded calico dress; there was a rip at her waist and Kincaid noticed how she tried to hide it with her arm. Her jet-black hair was loosely braided, and there was a light smudge on her short, turned-up nose.

While she was speaking, Deal had kept his eyes right on her, but she had not looked at him. Matt felt that the girl was avoiding his glance.

Conway now turned to the boy. "Well, young man, maybe you can add to that?"

The boy had been picking his nose. Now he stopped and whipped off his cap, his light yellow hair spilling in every direction like cornsilk; then he replaced the cap, the big bill low on his frowning forehead. He continued to look at the window and said nothing.

8

Kincaid looked across at Conway. "I'd say it could be Owl Creek, sir. Mr. Deal mentioned that there were two big mounds and that the creek was wide."

"That I did," said Deal impatiently.

"Any sign that they might have followed you, Mr. Deal?" Conway asked.

"Can't say. Nothing I noticed. And I kept a sharp lookout, figuring they might."

After a short pause, Conway pushed away from his desk. "I don't think we should talk anymore now, Mr. Deal. You've all three been through a very difficult experience. I have given orders for the guest barracks to be readied for you and your children, and you could probably use some food and drink." Conway stood up.

"Obliged, Captain Conway," Deal said, rising. The girl and boy followed suit, while Kincaid crossed to the door and opened it.

"But, Captain, I want satisfaction, not more talk. By God, two encounters with them redskins is enough. Hellfire, in Nebraska they wiped out the whole wagon train, save me an' them two!"

Conway's Virginia accent softened his words, and Matt admired his patience. "Mr. Deal, the army is here to protect emigrants—among its other duties—and you may rest assured that we fully intend to do so. A patrol will be sent out to investigate the whole situation." He looked at Kincaid.

"I'd like to take Windy with me, sir," Matt said.

"Just what I had in mind, Matt," Conway said. "And, uh, I think you could take Mr. Deal along too."

"What you want me for?"

"We need you to show us the way," Matt said. He grinned pleasantly, but there was no response from Deal.

"Get some rest, Mr. Deal," Conway said. "We'll call you when the patrol is ready. Meanwhile, you and your children make yourselves comfortable."

Ethan Deal had been on his way out the door, but now he stopped in his tracks and turned back toward Conway and Kincaid.

There was no change in his expression as he said, "'Preciate your hospitality, Captain." Those hot, metallic eyes fastened on the girl and boy. "That there is Nellie. T'other one I call Zack. Don't know his real name, on account of he don't never speak. They ain't my kids."

Dropping those words into the room, Ethan Deal ushered the girl and boy out, then followed them.

Conway, closing the door behind them, suddenly realized that the drop of water that had hung so long on the end of Ethan Deal's nose had fallen; but he hadn't seen it happen.

two _____

There were six of them, and they passed slowly
through the camp, talking to the people they encountered—old men sitting before their lodges smoking,
women at the cookfires. A small band of children followed them, their eyes big with awe, speechless as they
watched every move the men made; the youngsters were
half on the verge of laughter, half afraid of the men's
mysterious costumes, their strange behavior.

"Goodbye," said one of the men, greeting an old
woman at her fire where there was a pot of stew.

The woman said, "Would you have some stew to eat?"

"No, I don't want it," another said, piercing a piece
of stew meat on the end of his skinning knife. "Ah, it
is foul tasting," he said with a pleased smile on his face,
and smacking his lips with pleasure.

At another fire, a young woman was boiling water.
One of the six pulled up his long sleeve and plunged his
bare arm into the bubbling pot.

He leaped backward, almost knocking over one of the

children. "Ah—it is freezing cold!" Howling, shivering, he wrapped himself deeply into his robes while two of the other men started splashing each other with the steaming water, crying out how cold it was.

Dressed as women—in robes rather than breechclouts, with their hair not braided like that of warriors, but hanging loose like women's tresses—they walked backwards through the camp, while the children kept pace with their antics, and the eyes of the tribe followed them.

They were the Contrary Ones, members of the Dog Soldier Society who had undertaken to reverse all aspects of their lives and actions. As such, they were honored and given a special place in the tribe, for they were the fools who made fun of everything, even the highest things, and especially themselves.

Seated in front of his lodge, Faraway Eagle smoked his small clay pipe. His eyes looked straight ahead, but he was watching everything the Contraries did. He did not move, yet everything in him was fully alive in the stillness that emanated from him, the stillness that all— even the *veho*, the "spider people," the whites—noticed. He smoked, measuring everything, for it was the Cheyenne way never to hurry, though one needed always to be quick; quick yet not hurried, in order to do things well.

The chief was an old man now, and many snows had fallen upon his head. He was old enough to know that the true name of his people, the Cheyenne, was *Tsis-tsis-tas*, meaning the "True People," or the "Gashed People." He was old enough to know that long before his own time, that had been their first name.

Many, many winters—almost as far back as the time when the *Tsis-tsis-tas* had known no other humans, only themselves—Sweet Medicine had talked to the people, telling them:

I shall not be with you long now. Before I go, I have something to tell you. A time is coming when you will meet other people, and you will fight with them and will kill each other. Each tribe will want the land of the other tribe, and you will be fighting always.

Sweet Medicine, so the story went, then pointed toward the south and said, *Far away in that direction is another kind of buffalo, with long hair hanging down its neck, and a tail that drags on the ground; an animal with a round hoof, not split like a buffalo's, and with teeth in the upper part of its mouth as well as below. This animal you shall ride on. The buffalo will disappear, and when they have gone, the next animal you will have to eat will be spotted.*

Sweet Medicine had warned of other things: *Soon you will find among you people who have hair all over their faces, whose skin is white. When that time comes you will be controlled by them. The white people will be all over the land, and at last you will disappear.*

And then Sweet Medicine was gone; but the people remembered his words, and in time all of his prophecies except the last one came true.

So the Grandfathers had told Faraway Eagle in his vision when he was a boy of ten summers and winters. And so the elders—Wolf Running and Little Robe and Knife—had told him.

Yet now his heart was always heavy, for he feared constantly for the True People, lest not even one survive to remember. He feared now, more than ever, with the news of the white man's dead mule and how Running Bull had been shot. He had not been wounded seriously, but the incident had fanned the long-smoldering anger in the camp, for Running Bull was one of the Holy Ones. He was a contrary.

Faraway Eagle sat a long time in front of his lodge, feeling himself into the real world, praying in his heart for a way to help the people survive. From his neck hung the big silver peace medal given him by the President in *Wah-shah-tung*. It shone softly on his dark breast.

Matt Kincaid felt the power of the big bay gelding under him as he rode through the chill that held the plain in the hour before dawn. With him were Windy Mandalian, Ethan Deal, and Privates Malone and Gatwin. He was especially pleased to have Windy, Easy Company's chief scout, with him, for they had both fully agreed with Conway that there was something a bit off about Ethan Deal's story.

"He's lying, I'm sure of it," the captain had said when they discussed the situation just after Deal and the youngsters left his office.

"I had the definite feeling he wasn't giving out the whole story." Matt had shaken his head reflectively. "He's a strange bird. I'd like to find out just who those two children are, and what Deal is doing alone out here. Did he come all the way in that beaten-up wagon with a couple of half-dead mules? Or what?"

"That's why I really want you to take him along with you and Windy," Conway had explained. "Deal isn't the kind who likes to be questioned out-and-out. I mean he isn't going to talk straight. The man is a graveyard. But if you're riding with him, then he might give out something. Meanwhile, the youngsters—I don't know that I can refer to Nellie as a child, exactly—will be here with Ben Cohen and myself, and maybe Flora. You follow me? Might get something out of them."

Matt found himself grinning. "I do follow you, sir. I follow you especially about not thinking of Nellie as a child."

Conway broke into a laugh. Then he became serious again. "What did Deal mean about the boy not speaking?

Is he mute? And where did the two of them come from, if they're not his?"

"Maybe they're orphans, and Deal being a self-styled man of God . . ." Matt let it hang, spreading his hands, shrugging.

Conway's eyebrows lifted toward his hairline as he reached for his box of cigars. After helping himself, he pushed the box toward his adjutant, who declined with a small shake of his head.

Settling back, he bit off the little bullet of tobacco at the tip of his cigar, and struck a match. "Matt," he said, holding the lighted match in his hand, "we don't want the tribes attacking emigrant trains. That's what I'm really concerned with. If Deal shot a Cheyenne, it isn't going to help anything, damn it." He put the flaming match to the end of his cigar and puffed it alight.

"I understand, sir. I feel exactly the same way. And it seems that Regiment does too." He nodded toward the paper Conway had just picked up from his desk.

Conway nodded grimly, tapping the dispatch with his finger. "More trouble than the Little Bighorn and Sand Creek put together is what we can look for. There's a big wagon train supposed to be coming in up north by Crazy Woman Creek, and Regiment wants us to escort them. It's going to leave us shorthanded if we get many more." He paused. "But they'll be going on through to Oregon. We've also got a growing problem with squatters, as you know."

Matt nodded. "And whiskey, sir. Both Deal and the girl said they thought those Indians had been drinking."

Conway pointed his cigar at the wall map across from his desk. "Regiment's dispatch mentions squatters up near the north fork of the Sweetwater. You might take a look-see. They're apparently up close to tribal territory and not too far from where Deal lost his mule." He frowned. "Of course, as long as they're on federal land, there's not much we can do, providing they behave themselves—even though they're supposed to have homestead papers, which many of them don't."

Matt had shrugged at this. "Well, sir, we can give them the standard warning and tell them to file a claim. As you know, we don't get much backing for anything stronger than that. Trouble is, sir, sometimes they attract the riffraff."

"Just about always, I'd say." Conway had looked down at the back of his hand. "The Cheyenne are not going to like all these squatters, Matt; and this situation with Deal's mule doesn't help."

Later, Ben Cohen had suggested Kincaid take the new recruit, Gatwin, on patrol.

"He's a good man, Lieutenant. Pretty young, green but willing. Thing is, he needs seasoning, and if the lieutenant agrees, sir, I thought him and Malone might make a good pair." The first sergeant had grinned, seeing the slight surprise on Kincaid's face. "Malone's good with new recruits, sir, so long as they stay out of town."

Matt nodded. "That's for sure. Malone is a good soldier, and I like your suggestion, Sergeant."

"Yessir." And Ben Cohen, lord and master of the enlisted men of Easy Company—and, Matt was thinking, also mother hen—saluted briskly and moved off to assign the new recruit and the veteran, Malone, who hadn't a brain in his head as far as sensible living went, but was one of the best soldiers ever to sit a McClellan saddle. He could be just what young Gatwin needed to bring him right to the mark. And Matt Kincaid, watching the first sergeant crossing the parade, appreciated once again Ben Cohen's way of working his men.

Now the patrol had ridden hard through the predawn, Kincaid and Windy both concerned with reaching the place of Deal's confrontation with the Indians while there might still be fresh sign.

Windy—"all hair and buckskin," as Conway had once described him—rode easy in his saddle, almost as though there were no difference between himself and his little roan horse. Except—again according to Conway—the roan didn't chew tobacco.

The scout, studying the sky now, announced, "Comes to wettin' some, we'll find damn little sign."

"We'll hope it holds off," Matt said as they rode almost stirrup-to-stirrup down a long draw.

"Draw like this generally puts me in mind of Crazy Horse," the scout said, suddenly spitting in the direction of a jackrabbit sitting just off the trail.

Matt waited for him to say more, and when no further words were forthcoming, he turned toward his companion. "Why so?" he asked.

"Heard it from a scout name of Kicking Water. Crazy Horse, when it so happened he was being chased, used to run his horses downhill and slow 'em to a walk when climbing. That way, no one never got within shooting distance." He paused, spitting once again, getting some tobacco juice on the roan's withers, but neither he nor the animal paid any attention to it.

And again the riders fell into silence, with only the creaking of leather and the bright jangling of bits, the soft whisper of grass against the quick hooves of the horses. Now and again the riders were awarded the rank odor of Windy's cut-plug as he spat, always careful that the expectoration was downwind.

Ethan Deal proved to be no horsebacker and he was having trouble keeping up with the army, especially aboard the agonizing McClellan saddle he'd been issued. But he was tough; he held his tongue, riding behind Matt and Windy and ahead of Malone and Gatwin. He had lost some of his anger now, and was mainly concerned with staying on his horse and keeping up with the others.

When they rounded a low cutbank, a flock of geese swept across the sky as the tip of the sun moved above the horizon. Now the light penetrated the whole of the sky and the wide land beneath it. In another twenty minutes they topped a draw and rode toward the two low buttes that Deal had described.

"This it?" Windy asked, shifting his long, loose body in his battered stock saddle.

"That be it." Ethan Deal shifted in his saddle too, but uneasily. "I mind the old proverb, 'You can't judge a hoss by its saddle.' Praise be for that, or this beast would be in condition for the funeral pyre."

"Rough on the old balls, eh, Preacher Deal?" Windy squinted at the New Englander with a suspicion of a grin on his weatherbeaten face.

Matt realized the scout was trying to bait the farmer into opening up.

"Told you I ain't no preacher man, Scout. I be simply a simple man of the Lord."

"If you're gonna stay out in this here country," Windy went on, "you better learn 'bout settin' on a horse."

"I be a farmer," Deal said, and his voice was deep with conviction and reprimand for Windy Mandalian. "I ain't a man for gallivantin' around the country bustin' his privates on a animal that'd best be workin' before a plough. That's by God what a hoss is for—working!"

It was about the longest speech he had made since leaving Conway's office, and one of the least unpleasant, though his face maintained its same grim expression.

Windy and Matt and the two enlisted men swung out of their saddles. Deal was slower. "He comes down off that animal in sections," the scout muttered to Kincaid.

Windy and Matt started instantly looking for sign, while Malone and Gatwin watered the horses.

18

"You recollect anything else about the Indians?" Windy asked Deal.

"Only what I said—and more than oncet. They was peculiar, some of them looking like women, only they was men. Funny actions and way of talking."

"Might be Contraries," Windy said without looking up from the print he was studying. He was squatting, motionless, as he listened to Deal and also studied the footprint. "On the other hand, they could've been drunk as owls."

"What the hell is Contraries?" Deal asked.

"Like a smoke, Mr. Deal?"

"I don't mind if I do," Deal said, accepting the cigar Kincaid offered him.

When they had lighted up, Deal said, "I asked you what was Contraries, scout."

"They're sort of a secret society," Matt explained.

Windy had risen and now walked over to where they were standing. "Yup, it was them. You can tell by the moccasin prints. They was walking backwards. And one was hit in the right leg," he added, his eyes on Ethan Deal. "Pretty good shooting in the dark," he said. And then he added, "I mean if you was aimin' at his leg." And he stared at the feisty New Englander dead-center, his tongue bulging his cheek as though he had a ball in it.

Ethan Deal sniffed the whole length of his long nose, and leaned those hard, pewter-colored eyes on Windy Mandalian. "One of these days, after I get my horse, you an' me'll have us a shootin' contest."

"Good enough," Windy said.

"I could use me a extra hoss," Deal said, looking at the scout's little roan. Suddenly his face tightened. "You still ain't told me who them Contraries is. Those red devils was drunk as pissants is what I am saying!"

Windy took his time, taking out fresh cut-plug and

slicing off a sizable chew with his skinning knife, then working it around in his jaws to juice up the flavor. "They do everything the wrong way around," he said finally. "Like eat with their left hands, if they're right-handed, say yes when they mean no, wear women's clothes instead of men's. Like that."

"What they do that for?" Deal asked. "That sounds real crazy to me."

"They do everything backwards," Matt said.

"Backwards!"

"I heered they even fart backwards," Windy said, and he lowered his left eyelid over his eye, while keeping the right eye wide open. "They are plumb crazy!"

"It's a religious society," Matt explained.

"Religious!" Deal roared with indignation. "By jingo, they sound like the devil to me. That I will say!"

"The Contraries are considered holy people, I believe," Windy said.

"Holy!" Deal's great eyebrows shot straight up. "A bunch of godless heathen, I'll allow—to the last man, woman, and nit. I heered what Colonel Chivington done at Sand Creek, and I praise the Lord for him and his."

"Chivington, Mr. Deal, was a butcher." Matt said the words as calmly as though he were dealing a cool hand of poker. And he was pleased at himself for not letting his anger take over. He had listened to plenty of people like Ethan Deal, and neither he nor any frontier veterans had much stomach for their romantic nonsense.

"Godless animals!" roared Deal, raising his rusty-looking forefinger to heaven, perhaps to invoke power against the heathen, Matt thought ruefully.

"Let's take a look at that dead animal over yonder," Windy broke in.

"That be Jessie!" snapped Deal, stepping briskly forward, but still bent, with his elbows whipping out from his sides like wings. "Them red devils!"

"But it was yourself shot Jessie," Windy said as they stood over the animal."

"On their account, by God! I told the lieutenant and the captain a hundred times!"

"Pretty scrawny animal," Windy said, speaking slowly. Matt looked quickly at him. He knew the scout, knew by his tone that he was leading up to something. And then he looked closer at the mule and he saw what it was.

"You claim you shot this here mule by mistake when you was driving off your visitors?" Windy said carefully.

"That is so!"

"Bullshit!"

A taut silence fell over them as Deal's face went white. "What the hell are you saying, by God!" The sound that came out of the New Englander was like a knife blade scraping across a piece of iron.

"I mean, mister, that your mule there was dead 'fore she was shot."

"What the hell d'you mean by that!" But the scout had scored a bullseye. Kincaid watched the color change swiftly in Deal's face, turning from white to gray, and now whipping into flaming red.

"I am meaning," said Windy, speaking even slower, "that old Jessie there was dead before you shot her, on account of that gunshot wound which you claimed killed her didn't bleed."

Windy stood there squinting at the New Englander with his left eye closed, his bony jaws working vigorously on his tobacco. "Wouldn't be too surprised if it was on account of starvation that poor old Jessie cashed in. By God, she's scrawnier than the ass on a reamed-out prairie dog."

He held his eyes right on Deal all this while, but the farmer couldn't take it. He looked away. Then, hooking his hands in his galluses, he made a big effort to stand

21

up straight. But his long, curved body wouldn't obey. Matt and Windy both saw the glitter in his eyes as the pain, or whatever it was, hit him with the effort.

"Shit," he muttered, and he relighted his cigar. All at once his face cleared and there was something pretty close to a smile around his eye sockets and mouth as he said, "Shit, just engaging in a little Yankee horse trading. Might do them savages some good to learn something about sensible business."

"And it might do you some good," said Kincaid, "to learn that those savages are human beings."

"I still want protection through this territory, and I want my hoss!" Deal whipped the cigar out of his mouth. "Whether or not poor old Jessie was dead 'fore she was shot is not the point. It just ain't the point! She more'n likely died of a heart attack when them red heathen bastards come screaming at us. Yup—that is what must've happened! Her heart gived out." His mouth widened suddenly in a kind of grimace as he revealed brown, craggy teeth.

Kincaid wondered whether he was grinning or reacting to some inner pain.

Windy, in the meantime, had gone back to looking for sign, and was now studying the ground near a large clump of sagebrush. "They're Cheyenne for sure, Matt," he said. He straightened up and looked at Kincaid directly. "Figure it might make sense to pay a call on Faraway Eagle?"

Matt nodded. "That I do. And anyway, it's what the captain ordered." He lifted his head. "Private Malone."

"Yessir." Malone snapped out of his daydream and approached swiftly.

"Malone, you and Gatwin are to accompany Mr. Deal to Number Nine. Windy and I will be riding to Faraway Eagle's camp. You are to inform Captain Conway of that."

22

"Yessir."

"Lieutenant, I want to go along and get my hoss," Deal said angrily. "We've been wasting time, dammit!"

"Sorry, Mr. Deal, but we feel you'd not be very safe in the Cheyenne camp, since you did shoot one of them."

"You get my horse, Lieutenant."

"Mr. Deal," Matt said, looking straight at the New Englander, "I think I can assure you that you'll get what's coming to you, sir."

Windy, who had been standing near Matt, studying the toe of his boot, now raised his head to eject an enormous amount of tobacco and spittle onto the High Plains of Wyoming.

three —————————————

Captain Warner Conway sat reading the message that had just come over the wire from regimental headquarters. In effect, the news was that his mother-in-law, Mrs. Dodgson, had arrived at Regiment and would be coming on to Outpost Number Nine the following day.

"Shit," muttered the captain to nobody in particular, since he was by himself. He looked across his office to the map on the opposite wall.

"Damn," he said, louder this time. Leaning back in his easy chair, he took a long drag on his cigar. "Shit," he said again and rose, and, still holding the dispatch, walked out into the orderly room. Ben Cohen looked up from his desk.

"Sergeant, you've read this?"

"Yes, sir, I have."

In the short pause that followed, the two men exchanged glances.

"Have Bradshaw return a message to Regiment that I am obliged to Regiment for courtesy toward Mrs. Dodgson, etcetera, etcetera...hell, you know how to write it better than I do." Conway broke off grumpily, and turned his head to gaze out the window.

"Yes, sir," Cohen said smartly. "Corporal Bradshaw," he called across the room, and the company clerk rose from his desk in the corner and approached swiftly.

Cohen looked sympathetically at his commanding officer. He was thinking that this explained Conway's irritability the past day or two. The captain was seldom out of sorts, and usually in good humor, but lately Ben Cohen, who had served under him all these years, had seen that Warner Conway's good nature was under siege. And after all, he reflected, how would he feel if Maggie Cohen's mother were suddenly to visit them at Outpost Nine? Biddie Brogan—massive, eternally garrulous, inflexible, rising before him in imagination right there in the orderly room—caused him to break out in a sweat.

Ben Cohen's great heart went out to Warner Conway, for *his* mother-in-law was in fact coming to Number Nine. It was hard to believe, somehow—Captain Warner Conway with a mother-in-law. But Cohen was a realist. He understood fully that between the possibility of the hostiles hitting the path again and the actuality of the imminent arrival of Flora Conway's mother at Outpost Number Nine, the captain was in trouble. Indeed, Cohen reflected, they all were.

"Mrs. Dodgson will probably be driven over in the ambulance, sir."

"Yes, tomorrow," Conway said, looking down at the dispatch, his voice hollow.

"We'll keep a close contact with Regiment, sir."

Conway nodded somewhat vaguely, and started toward the door. He had decided that he needed a drink, and Flora's pleasant company. It might be their last evening alone for some time; Mavis Dodgson had written that she would look forward to visiting with them for

26

"quite a while." Those words had put a chill into Conway's blood.

And yet, he told himself as he crossed the parade—and truthfully—it wasn't that he disliked the old lady. Actually, she was quite nice, he enjoyed her company; they'd even had fun together on occasion. She enjoyed her whiskey. No, it was just the matter of having her at Outpost Number Nine—a nice woman, but one who saw her daughter still as "my little girl," a phrase that curdled Conway's innards. And Mrs. Dodgson was one of the great conversationalists of all history. Quite simply, Mavis Dodgson knew everything. And there was never the slightest hesitation on her part in indicating that fact to everyone she encountered.

Thank God, Flora sympathized with him. In fact, she agreed with her husband's summation of the situation, and had tried to dissuade her mother from the visit, pointing out its disadvantages: the discomfort of frontier travel, the problems of life on a frontier army post, and the hazards of the hostile neighbors. All to no avail. They might have known! The more the inconveniences were indicated to Mavis Dodgson, the more determined she became to "overcome" them. The woman was a warrior; no question.

Crossing the parade in the hot morning sunshine, Warner Conway was so engrossed in imagining the presence of Flora's mother at Outpost Number Nine that he almost ran into the small boy, who seemed suddenly to appear from nowhere. There he was, that great shock of yellow hair spilling out from beneath the battered cap with its huge bill, the face turned up all fresh, freckled, and grinning—with two teeth missing—to greet the commanding officer's height. And—by jiminy!—up whipped a blinding salute, razor-sharp, that all but knocked the saluter off his stride. Warner Conway, completely surprised, could only return the salute in his best military

27

manner, which was by no means up to his usual standard.

They were past each other in a flash. Conway wanted more than anything to turn and look at the boy, but he didn't dare. He was left with a sense of his own discomfiture at being so caught off guard, and with a great urge to break into laughter at the sight of that freckled, grinning face. Almost shaking with the effort to hold himself equal to the encounter, he made it to his quarters, where, on closing the door behind him, he burst into uncontrollable mirth.

Flora Conway, emerging from the bedroom, stared at her husband in amazement. "Warner, what ever has happened? Have you and Windy Mandalian been drinking?"

"My dear, I have just witnessed the answer to the whole bloody situation between Indians and whites." And he described to her the scene with young Zachary on the parade.

"I wish I'd seen it," Flora said.

"The thing is, he doesn't speak. He's never said a word that anybody's heard, at any rate. But what a gesture!"

They had seated themselves on the sofa, and Conway leaned back, shaking his head, his eyes still dancing with laughter. But then, suddenly remembering how badly Flora and he had wanted children, he stopped.

She felt the change in him, knowing why. "Warner, dear man," she said, sitting up, "one good gesture deserves another. I am, of course, speaking of a drink!"

"A delightful thought, Mrs. Conway." He stood up. "Might I do the honors for the most delightful lady in the whole world?"

"And for the most delicious man," she said, her eyes softly teasing him.

"Flora!"

She became all innocence. "Why, Warner, did I say something I shouldn't?"

For a long moment he stood there looking down at her, holding her gaze; but she couldn't keep that expression of innocence, and soon they were laughing in each other's arms.

"I think this evening we should have our drinks horizontally, my dear." And she nibbled lightly on his earlobe while he thought he would lose his sanity.

"Flora..."

"You're not going to scold me, are you, Warner?" She was lying beneath him, looking up into his eyes, which were only inches away. "I do love to tease you...a little bit."

"You do an excellent job of teasing me," he said happily. "Perhaps you wouldn't mind a little turnabout. Perhaps I could tease you."

"I agree. Oh, I do agree!"

He began to undress her while he kissed her eyes, her ears, her lips, and, at last, when her breasts were exposed, her nipples.

"Warner, your belt buckle. Couldn't we be demilitarized for a moment?"

"But of course, Mrs. Conway. Anything for a lady." And he half rose so that she could help him take off his trousers.

They were naked now, and together they rolled off the sofa and onto the rug. He entered her easily as she spread her thighs eagerly to receive him.

The sign was sloppily painted, the black paint having dripped in many places from the broad, carelessly formed letters, which read: JELLICOE CITY—PRIVAT PLAICE—KEEP OUT! P. JELLICOE, PROP.

Matt and Windy drew rein. "Welcome to the north fork of the Sweetwater," Windy said laconically, spitting in the direction of the board sign that had been nailed to a cottonwood tree. They had just crossed a clearing and were about to follow the trail through the trees on the other side.

"Must be the squatters," Matt said. And he suddenly realized that Windy was sitting absolutely still on the little roan.

"I do believe our host is right near us, Matt," the scout said. "And he don't feel very welcoming to me."

Slowly Matt turned his head just at the moment that six men stepped into the clearing. Each was carrying a rifle, and each had one or two sixguns strapped at his side.

"You gents looking for something?" asked the eldest among them.

"No," said Matt, taking his time. "We live here. What are you, who are you, and what's that sign doing there?"

The man had a long, flowing, heavily stained beard, sharp little eyes set close together, and clothes torn almost to the point of rags. He was dirty. He wore a single suspender crossways from his left hip over his right shoulder.

"This is Jellicoe land here, mister soldier. That's what that sign is doin' there. We don't want no Injuns, no squatters, nor..." He spat swiftly, barely turning his head, and almost hitting one of his companions. "Nor no army."

"Your name Jellicoe?" Matt said.

"It be."

"And the others?"

"Their names be Jellicoe too. We is family, Purvis Jellicoe being yours truly, and his five sons—Porter, Print, Prior, Palmer, and Poon. Now what kin we do for you, mister soldier?"   .

"As far as I know, this is federal land you're on here, Mister Jellicoe. You have a cabin or something?"

"Got a soddy yonder," throwing his head back over his shoulder. "Federal land, you say. Shit, the government says we citizens can move onto federal land and work it. And that is what we are doing. And we don't need no fucking interference from the fucking army."

"You are also mighty close to tribal land here—in this case, Cheyenne," Matt said.

"Don't give a shit," said the elder Jellicoe. "Do you, boys?"

The five guffawed at the thought of giving a shit about tribal land.

"You have papers for this land, Mr. Jellicoe?"

"Yup. That we do." And he reached into his shirt and brought out a dirty, folded paper. "If you'll be good enough to ride over here, mister soldier—my old feet is killing me—why, I'll be proud to show it you."

Matt threw a glance to Windy, and kicked his bay horse forward. Reaching down, he accepted the paper from Jellicoe.

"Got any whiskey in Jellicoe City?" he asked, handing the paper back.

"Nary a drop."

"Keep it that way, Mr. Jellicoe."

"What the hell you mean, mister soldier!"

Kincaid's eyes glinted as he looked at Jellicoe dead center. "I mean this. That paper doesn't mean a thing. We don't encourage squatters here, so I am telling you—no, I am warning you; one smell of trouble and the army will jump right up your ass. You understand me?"

"I understand you." Jellicoe said it hard, but he knew he'd pushed as far as he could.

Matt lifted his reins. "And one more thing—the name is Lieutenant Kincaid. I expect you to remember that, Mr. Jellicoe."

As they rode off, Matt said to Windy, "Well, what do you think, old scout?"

Windy let his face fall into a slow grin before speaking. "I think you done right good, Matt. 'Case you're interested in knowin' who you braced there, that was Paw Jellicoe and his boys."

"I know that."

"But do you know that that sweet old pappy used to ride with Quantrill and Bloody Bill Anderson?"

"Jesus, no wonder he's so friendly to union soldiers."

Windy chuckled. "You handled that coyote son of a bitch just right, Matt. I am proud of you."

"So he was one of the Quantrill bushwhackers."

"A sweetheart."

"And his boys?"

Windy stuck out his lower lip. "They are his boys."

four ─────────────

More than thirty winters. Ah, there had been many changes. Faraway Eagle sat looking into the small buffalo-chip fire. More than thirty winters since the Cheyenne saw the first wagon train of emigrants go up the Oregon Trail. And the wise ones had known it was the beginning of the end of their way of life.

It had seemed almost no time before a river of wagons was pouring across the land, spoiling the good grass, killing off the buffalo, cutting down the scant wood along the creeks.

Soon there had come reports that the Kiowa, Comanche, Apache, Arapaho, Pawnee, and Sioux were attacking the wagon trains, and the emigrants were crying to *Wah-shah-tung* for protection. The True People had stayed out of the trouble as much as possible; only now and again angry young men eager to fight against the *veho* and prove themselves, ran off to take part in a raid. The tribe might as well have gone along, for in the long run they were blamed anyhow.

Faraway Eagle had been at the great peace meeting at Horse Creek those many winters past, when the Cheyenne met with eight other tribes, which included their traditional foes, the Crows and the *Ho-he*—the latter called Assiniboine by the whites. At the meeting the Cheyenne had willingly "touched the pen" while a white man wrote their names on the paper. The True People were surely for peace.

Yet it was as though nothing could bring peace. That same year the *veho* emigrants brought the sickness to the Platte, what the whites called cholera, and following that came the sickness with the terrible spots, killing thousands from all the tribes. Everywhere was misery. Surely there would be no going back to the Shining Times.

Still, there were old men who spoke for peace with the *veho*. But the old counselors had not always managed to keep the young hotheads under control. There seemed always to be some 'incident," some excuse for the fighting. And the peace chiefs, those who tried to keep their people together—as he, Faraway Eagle had tried to do—were in a losing struggle.

All this—failure and bitterness, frustration and fury—was there in the camp of Faraway Eagle when, just before noon, Matt Kincaid and Windy Mandalian rode in.

"It is for sure not the great party of the year," Windy said to Matt in a low voice as they rode slowly past the stolid faces, whose very lack of expression was more threatening than any physical gesture.

Kincaid's tone was rueful. "I'd agree that our hosts are not feeling too friendly toward us."

When they dismounted in front of the chief's lodge, there was a slight movement toward them from the nearest onlookers. But at a word from a Dog Soldier policeman, the onlookers grew still, though their anger seemed to mount in the new silence.

But then the muttering started up once more in the crowd of Cheyenne, and some of them pressed forward in spite of warnings from the Dog Soldiers.

Windy had just started to say something to the Cheyenne crowding around them when Faraway Eagle stepped out of his lodge, and the muttering and gesticulating subsided. But the atmosphere of hostility did not.

"Greetings, Lieutenant and friend Windy," the chief said. "It is fortunate for all of us that the Cheyenne custom is to treat with courtesy all who enter our camp."

"Faraway Eagle, we have come to talk," Matt said, at the same time appreciating the chief's sardonic sense of humor. "We wish to show our open hand to you." And Matt held out both his hands with the palms up.

"We will smoke first," Faraway Eagle said. And he spoke in Cheyenne to one of his headmen.

Now a young brave brought a blanket and the chief sat down crosslegged. His headmen seated themselves, forming a circle with Faraway Eagle, and including Matt and Windy.

Carefully the pipe was prepared, offered to the Four Directions, to the Above and the Below, and then passed.

Faraway Eagle spoke. "I see that you have come in peace, Lieutenant and Windy. It is good."

"We wish to keep peace with the Cheyenne," Kincaid said.

"That I know. You have come about the shooting of Running Bull and, too, about the white men coming so many here. The men with the wagons."

"We have also come about the selling of whiskey. We know you do not wish it for your people, but we have heard that it is being brought into the territory."

Faraway Eagle nodded once, his hand moving his

eagle-wing fan. "I have only heard talk of the whiskey, Lieutenant. But it is the wagon people who bring it. There are some new people at Gooseberry Creek, what you call the north fork of the Sweetwater."

"We were just there," Matt said.

After a moment Faraway Eagle said, "I trust you, Lieutenant and Windy." His eyes looked into the distance. "But you are two. And there are many, many whites. And Running Bull has been shot by the man in the black hat. Fortunate it is that he was not killed."

"It was a bad thing, and the man is sorry," Kincaid said. "It was a mistake. The man had been in a rubout of his wagon train and he had two children with him. He thought the warriors had come to steal his mules."

"But he lied. The mule he tried to trade was dead."

"The army will repay what damage you feel is right, Faraway Eagle."

"But what about Running Bull?" asked one of the headmen seated in the circle. "Our men were not armed, and yet his man shot at them."

"Ho!" the others said in agreement.

"It is done," Windy said. "And the army will try to make it up to you."

There followed another silence. Some of the Cheyenne began talking among themselves. Faraway Eagle said nothing. He smoked, waiting.

Now, from the warriors standing behind the circle, came a rumbling.

"What are they saying?" Matt asked Windy.

"They ain't happy."

"I don't need the Great Scout of the Western Plains to tell me that," Kincaid replied sardonically.

"They want Deal," Windy said.

"Enough!" The word came from Faraway Eagle, and it was spoken with power. The Cheyenne seldom spoke other than softly, and while Faraway Eagle's voice kept

36

this quality of softness, it had a power in it that seemed stronger because its strength was not harsh, but couched in just that softness. "Young men, you must not forget where you are," he admonished sternly.

He turned his head toward the white men again. "It is not so easy, Lieutenant. This man shot his rifle at our people who were carrying no guns, and had not come prepared for fighting. Clearly the man was trying to cheat them, for his horse—the mule—was already dead."

"*Ho! Ho!*" said the voices in the circle.

"And then he shot Running Bull and would perhaps have shot and killed others if he had been able."

The warriors standing behind the circle started to murmur loudly now, and Faraway Eagle raised his arm; he was holding the pipe from which those who were seated had smoked.

"As you know, Windy and Lieutenant, the Contrary Ones are of the Dog Soldier Society, and we must hear from them to see what must be done. For this man has shot a Cheyenne, a member of the Dog Soldier Society, and a Contrary. True, the bullet did not kill. But it is the Dog Soldiers and the Contrary Ones who must decide what is to be done. I have spoken."

The chief's English was precise and carefully modulated, and Matt thought how well it sounded in the soft Cheyenne tone. Faraway Eagle added to the atmosphere of serenity with his gestures, which now and again added the sign language of the plains so that the Cheyennes present who did not speak English should understand what he was saying.

"I think that's the best we can do, Matt," Windy said, speaking low. "We're lucky we go this far. They're pretty damn mad."

"How long is this going to take, Windy?"

"They're talkin' about it now," Windy said, and nodded at some of the Dog Soldiers who were standing behind the circle of headmen. Several were speaking.

Meanwhile, Kincaid turned his head and watched Faraway Eagle, who sat so quietly he seemed to be asleep. The chief's gray hair fell in braids on his broad shoulders. A single eagle feather stood straight up from the back of his head.

At length one of the Dog Soldiers spoke, addressing the chief and the headmen. He spoke in Cheyenne, and Kincaid noted that everyone was listening attentively, but he realized suddenly that the Cheyenne were listening not at all the way whites did, with a certain tenseness to catch the words that might be missed, but rather by being absolutely immobile and without making a sound. He saw that it was this quality that had made him think Faraway Eagle had been asleep, when actually it was evident now that the old chief wasn't missing a thing.

Now Faraway Eagle turned his head toward the two white men. "Did you understand what Many Fires said?"

"They want the white man to stand trial; they say that is what would happen if a Cheyenne shot a white," Windy said.

Faraway Eagle was looking at Matt. "But I see that Lieutenant says no."

"We cannot do that," Matt said. "But we will pay what we can for Running Bull being wounded."

At this there was a loud burst of talking from the Dog Soldiers and Contraries.

"You see, Lieutenant and Windy," and there was a faint smile on Faraway Eagle's face, "the Contraries already knew your answer. For an Indian brought to white man's trial is killed; and so this white man fears that we would do the same."

"I do not make the law," Kincaid replied.

"That I know. But you see, the Contraries . . . you know they do things backwards. That is why they have

38

asked for justice from the white man. Of course they do not expect it."

Faraway Eagle suddenly began to speak in Cheyenne to his headmen and the Contraries.

"Ho!" the headmen said when he had finished. *"Ho!"*

After some moments, when the headmen and others had said *"Ho!"* many times, the Cheyenne named Many Fires spoke to Kincaid and Windy. "Running Bull's brother, Buffalo Shirt, will fight the white man of the mule with knives," he said, pointing to a young, powerful looking warrior. "Should Buffalo Shirt win, then the Contrary Ones need not give a horse, but they will take the live mule. But if the white man wins, then a horse will be given to him."

"That's not a fair fight," Matt said. "The white man with the mule is old. Buffalo Shirt is young and strong."

There was again a ripple of talk among the Cheyenne. Finally they were again silenced by Faraway Eagle.

"Very well," said Many Fires. "We will find someone to fight the man. But it must be agreed that before the next moon this matter of honor will be settled." Many Fires was a tall, solidly built man, no longer young, but certainly vigorous. He spoke his words to Faraway Eagle; and when he finished, a silence fell over the group as they awaited the chief's response.

"It is a good way," Faraway Eagle said. "Do you agree to it, Lieutenant?"

"I will speak to the white man," Matt said. "I understand that it is a thing of honor. And I will send you a message."

The chief rose to his feet and everyone followed suit. He stood straight in front of Kincaid and Windy Mandalian, a slight wind stirring the fringes on his buckskin tunic, the solitary feather on his head.

"You white men are many," he said, "and we are few.

39

You have many guns, many soldiers, much land that you say now is yours. We Cheyenne have only ourselves. We are few and you are many. But we will trust you."

five ━━━━━━━━━━━━━

Warner Conway, still vigorous in his middle for-
ties—and, if anyone had wanted to know, stronger sex-
ually than ever before—adored his wife. His wife adored
him, and moreover agreed that his sexuality left nothing
to be desired other than repetition. Both addressed themselves assiduously to this "problem." It wasn't only in
bed that they found pleasure in each other's company;
they not only loved, but liked each other very much. The
only thing they lacked was a child, but this desire had
passed and, as they both agreed, the absence of children
gave them more time for each other.

But the subject of children had been a sore point with
Flora's mother. That she was not going to become a
grandmother had become one of the great sorrows of her
life. Mavis Dodgson was a person who saw everything
in absolutes. To be childless was to be without a future.
On top of this, there was the question of her son-in-law's
being overage in grade. Why hadn't Warner been pro-

moted? He should have been a major years ago. What was wrong?

Flora had long since realized how useless it was to try explaining army red tape to her mother. In vain she had pointed out that the present government, under President Hayes, was still recoiling from the excesses of the previous administration, and so was on an economy drive; she had noted that Matt Kincaid, Warner's adjutant, was also overage in grade, and that Sergeant Ben Cohen, the company top kick, was in a similar position. Indeed, she could have cited numerous others in the army who suffered the same lack of recognition for their abilities.

These matters were seldom mentioned now, but they were there nonetheless, and both Conway and Flora realized that the subjects might very well be brought out in conversation, and would certainly be hovering in the background during the visit. Yet they were fond of Mavis Dodgson, and she liked her son-in-law in spite of his obvious shortcomings. The Conways had hoped to visit Mavis on Warner's next leave, but she had forestalled them by writing that she would visit them "in the field." It would be the first time she'd visited them at an army post, and she had written them how much she was looking forward to "the great adventure."

"It will only be for a short while," Flora had told her husband, but he was not mollified.

"Your mother's short while, my dear, is my eternity," he had said, and then laughed. "Say, that's not bad. Next time I have to make a speech, I'll remember that. In a different context, of course," he added.

"We'll just have to find things to keep Mother occupied," Flora said.

"I am afraid, my dear, that our problem will be to keep her *un*occupied," he sighed. He was sitting on the edge of their bed, pulling on his socks, while she sat nearby, brushing her long black hair.

"I just hope she doesn't start in on my not getting promoted."

"She won't."

"How can you be so sure?"

"We'll both see to it that she doesn't." Flora rose from the stool she'd been sitting on and put down her hairbrush. She was wearing a loose-fitting wrapper; it was early morning and they had both just awakened.

"Warner, you and I both know that if you did get your promotion, you'd be shipped out to another assignment; and it would be the same if Matt Kincaid got his captaincy. In either case, there'd be no more Easy Company as we know it. So, for myself, I'm perfectly happy the way things are."

Still seated on the edge of the bed, he reached out his hand, and she came forward and took it.

"You know you're a man who loves his job," she said. "It shows all over you."

He chuckled, his eyes shining on her as he drew her down beside him, squeezing her hand. "I am a man who loves his wife," he said simply. "I'm the luckiest man in the world."

"And I am the luckiest woman."

"Enough of this sentiment, young lady. Get that robe off! And that's an order!" He had made his voice extra gruff, as he grinned at her.

"You'd better get your socks off, young man."

"Consider them off," he said, reaching for them. He flung them across the room and then sat close, looking at her naked body, at her breasts hanging firm and almost touching him, and at the dark, curly hair between her legs.

"Whatever are you staring at, sir?"

"I am looking at heaven, and at that marvelous forest of miracles." He reached up and caressed the side of her face.

"Maybe . . . maybe you'd wish to accept an invitation to enter that forest?"

In one smooth movement he was on top of her as she lay back on the bed, her legs wide apart. "Never let it be said that Warner Conway failed to respond to an invitation from the captain's lady," he said. The words came out in a sigh of ecstasy.

He rode her gently, sweetly, and then he rode her hard, taking different positions, or rather they let their bodies take them, never missing a stroke. Now she was on top, and now he was behind her. And at last, building to the most exquisite encounter of all, he returned to mount her as he had at the start, their loins pumping in ecstatic rhythm until their orgasm released them.

They were still lying in each other's arms and legs, when there came a knock at the door. It was a while before he could respond. The knocking persisted, and suddenly he remembered he was in the army.

"Who is it?" he asked thickly.

"It's Corporal Bradshaw, sir," said the voice on the other side of the door. "Mrs. Dodgson has just arrived."

The day broke into a spectacular dawn, and when the thin call of Reb McBride's trumpet penetrated the fine air, it was as though the morning had been waiting for it. The day continued fine through breakfast and morning muster. In the mess hall, Sergeant Dutch Rothausen, the Germanic giant who attended to Easy Company's culinary needs, raged at his two KPs. Privates Gatwin and Malone, having just returned from patrol duty with Lieutenant Kincaid and Windy Mandalian, had drawn the detail— Gatwin because it was his turn, and Malone because of a backlog of punitive debt, of which First Sergeant Cohen always kept accurate notation. It was said that the Sarge never forgave or forgot. In any case, it

44

wouldn't have been easy to forget Malone, who was as large as Rothausen, and as ornery.

"I'm putting you back in the kitchen, Malone," Sergeant Cohen had told him, "even though I don't like Gatwin to get too much of your kind of army, but Sergeant Rothausen is shorthanded."

"Right, Sarge. I expected it."

"Maybe some day you'll work off all your back shit details, Malone."

"That would be great, Sarge."

"But I doubt you will. You're so dumb you'll get your finger in a bear trap 'fore you can scratch your own ass."

"Yes, Sarge."

Rothausen was not any kinder to the big Irishman. "Wouldn't you know I'd be saddled with you again! Shit, shit, shit!" But he put Malone to work on the big pots, and assigned Gatwin as his helper.

"It's on account of I do such a good job that I'm always on these details," Malone confided to the new man.

Gatwin was a good worker. He was clearly the youngest of the enlisted men, and he was no dummy. He worked hard, and he took orders well. He had, morever, a disarming frankness about him that won his colleagues over.

"I don't mind saying I was a bit scared when we were out there where those Indians had been. Do you get scared sometimes, Malone?"

"If you think any of us old-timers in the outfit don't get scared..." Malone said. "But you've got Matt Kincaid and Windy Mandalian, and they're your best argument in a fight with hostiles."

"I can see what you mean." Gatwin, a blond-headed youth, looked as though he could be still in school. He was interested in everything, and if anyone could find any fault with him, it would be just that—he was tireless in trying to learn everything about what was going on.

"How hot do you keep those ranges, Sergeant Rothausen?"

"Hot enough to burn your ass if you sit on 'em," came the brisk answer. "Now get to work, and stop all that bullshitting."

"Why do the Indians have Spencer repeaters while the army has Trapdoor Springfields?" was the question Gatwin put to Ben Cohen. Upon this particular question, the young man found that he had trod on one of Cohen's sore toes. The Indians—that is to say, the hostiles—had repeaters, but the army didn't.

"And where did these warriors get those repeaters?" asked the first sergeant, raising his weary eyes to heaven.

"Where did they, Sarge?" asked the eager Gatwin.

"They got them from the United States Government!"

"Why is that, Sarge?" asked Gatwin, his face exuding utter innocence. "I don't understand that."

A long sigh swept the full length of Ben Cohen's muscular body. His gaze, raised as though searching for heavenly guidance, now dropped to the young recruit standing attentively before him. Those eyes were kindly, the lids slightly lowered with excruciating patience as the soft, modulated voice enunciated the words carefully. "Private Gatwin, you ask why." Another sigh ran through that great body. "Tell me then, Private Gatwin, why there are so many more assholes in the world than there are asses!" The eyelids whipped back, and those great, red-streaked orbs sprang out like two great knobs. Under their frightening impact, Gatwin almost had to take a step backward.

"Sarge likes to get excited, doesn't he?" Gatwin confided later to Malone.

The Irishman grinned as he reached inside one of the big pots with a rag. "That he does, young feller."

46

"Stop that goddamn gabbing and get your asses moving!" The roar came from so close behind them that Malone almost dropped the big pot, and Gatwin jumped.

The fury at their rear was a flaming Dutch Rothausen. "I never did see two talkers like you knotheads, by God. Malone, you'd make someone a great wife, I don't mind tellin' you. Do you ever stop talking, Malone?"

"No, Sarge. I mean, yes, Sarge. I do."

"When? When you're asleep, I'll bet."

"Yes, Sarge."

"I bet he talks in his sleep!" Rothausen said, looking at Gatwin. "Do you talk in your sleep?" he asked Malone.

"I dunno, Sarge. Never had any complaints." And Malone gave a muffled chuckle into the big pot as he scrubbed.

Dutch Rothausen strode across the mess hall, his huge arms swinging at his side. Only Ben Cohen was bigger or tougher than the mess sergeant, but that was nothing for Rothausen to be ashamed of. Dutch Rothausen, it could be said, was a man of emotion. He had been known to cry with fury and frustration. Aroused—usually at the incompetence of kitchen help—he was a raging bull. Within the boundaries of his province he brooked no interference. After all, who was it that said an army travels on its stomach? Dutch understood the truth in that remark. "What would all you men do if you suddenly got bad food and had the shits, and the hostiles attacked?" he had often philosophized. "You better treat the mess hall with proper respect. You got the diarrhea from rotten cooking, you couldn't fight your way out of the nearest latrine." He shared one basic trait with Ben Cohen, and it was that, like Cohen, Rothausen's bark was *not* worse than his bite. Indeed, for the hapless enlisted man who fell out of favor with both Cohen and Dutch Rothausen, there was simply no place to go.

"That water ain't hot enough," he said, suddenly shoving past Malone and reaching into the big pot. "You want the men to get the shits, do you!"

Malone stepped back, wiping sweat from his steaming brow. "Sarge, I can hardly put my hands in that water."

Rothausen plunged his own bare forearm deep into the pot. "It's ice cold. You get that boiling."

"Sarge, there's bubbles on it now."

"Bullshit!" And Rothausen plunged his other immense hairy arm deep into the pot. Steam rose from the pot to envelop him. He stepped back while the two men ran their forearms across their brows, around which each had tied a kerchief.

Suddenly Private Gatwin, who had turned away from the sink, stared. He froze in his tracks. Was it a mirage? No, the figure was real enough, standing there in the doorway of the kitchen.

"Is this the kitchen?" asked the shrill, gargling voice.

"What the hell do you think it is, mister, and what are you doing here? State your business or get out!" demanded Dutch, without looking around.

Private Gatwin watched the figure detach itself from the doorway and stride toward Rothausen, who was soaking with perspiration as always, as much from agitation as from the heat in the kitchen.

"Is it Sergeant Ruthouse I am addressing?" The figure spoke to the broad, sweating back of Dutch.

"The name is Rothausen!" And Dutch wheeled on the intruder, spraying sweat in every direction as he did so.

A charged pause followed while the huge mess sergeant took in the short figure of the woman standing before him, wrinkling her nose.

"I am Mrs. Dodgson. I am Mrs. Conway's mother. I assume you are the person in charge of the mess?"

"I am the mess sergeant, madam. Sergeant Rothausen. Pleased to meet you, I'm sure." He spun suddenly on Malone and Gatwin, who were standing with their mouths hanging open. "What are you two gawking for! Ain't you never seen a lady before? Get to work!" And as though in response to the leonine roar, a pot lid slid off the counter and crashed to the floor. Before the furious Dutch could respond, Private Gatwin had swept it into his hand and returned it to the counter.

"Not there, you dummy! It's dirty. You got to wash it again!"

"Right, Sarge." And Gatwin addressed himself to the pot lid as though nothing else existed for him in the entire world.

"Sergeant, I am sure you won't mind if I take a look around the kitchen."

Neither Malone nor Gatwin turned to look at Rothausen—they wouldn't have dared—but they could feel the temperature rising behind them. The mess sergeant planted himself in all his authority in front of Mrs. Dodgson, the mother of the captain's wife, and the mother-in-law of the captain.

"Madam, you may inspect the kitchen. I do not mind. I mind nothing but my own business!" His words lowered the temperature of the kitchen several degrees. Having delivered this succinct bit of philosophy to the intruder, Sergeant Rothausen turned and strode out of the kitchen.

six ———————————

Windy Mandalian sat on the steps of the sutler's store, whittling a stick. The afternoon was dry, soft, the air still, the green and brown land spread out beneath a startling blue sky, a sky that looked as though it had just been minted. Windy was intent on his whittling, not even interrupting his deft knifework as he now and again ejected a stream of tobacco juice onto the parade.

The boy, Zack, was sitting on his heels on the ground watching him, his eyes shaded from the sun by the long bill of his cap.

"Why don't you speak none?" Windy asked. "You know, I ain't convinced you don't know how. I figure you just don't want to." He frowned goodnaturedly at his whittling. "Can't say I'd fault you for that."

He shifted his eye to the boy to catch his reaction, but there was none. The face was impassive, still soft beneath its freckles, the mouth just slightly open. Windy felt there was something expectant about him, almost as though he wanted to speak, yet couldn't find the right place or time.

"Want to whittle some?" He looked up now, studying the boy.

The big bill nodded. Under it, the blue eyes were round and wide. Suddenly he whipped off the cap and resettled it on his head, with that long bill lower than before. Then, leaning forward with one hand on the ground to support him, he reached out his other hand to accept the knife and the stick.

"Ever whittle?" Windy asked.

The boy was sitting again on his heels, with his eyes lowered to the barlow knife and the piece of wood.

"He don't speak—he don't never say nothin'." Ethan Deal's voice cut into the little tableau as he approached on his big feet, limping slightly. Windy couldn't tell whether the little limp was from pain or from some kind of attitude the strange man had toward life.

"Figgered that, by God," Windy said in response to Deal's observation on the boy's not talking. "How could you tell?"

Deal chose to ignore the scout's wry humor. "Found him and the girl down by Scott's Wells, Nebraska. They was in the Injun massacre, same as myself." He stared off over Windy's head. "Hell, it was. Burned bodies, wagons. What them red savages done would made the devil himself throw his guts."

"How come they didn't get the three of you?"

"Me, I was knocked down in the fightin'. They likely figgered me for dead. The kids, I dunno. Mebbe hiding. We were lucky." He paused, looking down at the ground. "Hester wasn't." His voice had suddenly gone hollow.

"Your wife?"

The big head, covered by the dirty black felt hat, nodded.

"So you brought them along with you, just like that."

"That is the size of it."

Windy had been watching the boy, who apparently had his whole attention fixed on his efforts at whittling.

"Me and my wife figgered we'd see the Oregon country." Reaching across his slumped chest with his left hand, Deal dug his fingers into his right armpit. "Don't guess I'll make it now."

"Why not?" Windy asked "Nothing stopping you here. You could take them with you." He nodded toward the boy. "Might prove useful, him and her both."

"I ain't cut out for nursemaiding. I figger to push along, only not to Oregon. Not that far."

"And leave them two here?"

"There ain't nothin' I kin do for 'em. 'Specially now. I only got me one half-assed mule. This goddamn army ain't worth a can of cold piss, far as gettin' that horse that's owed me."

Windy squinted at him. "I believe the lieutenant's gonna talk to you about that. He's been pretty busy since we got back. But I do believe he's got something on his mind about it."

Deal spat again, looking up at the sky. "'Debt hath a small beginning but a giant's growth and strength,'" he intoned.

"You could go back to Massachusetts, maybe," Windy said. "Get them two into school or somethin'. Maybe get some help for the boy there."

"Massachusetts is the devil's province. Me, I want to meet up with the Lord. I got some questions. I figure west is the direction."

Ethan Deal shoved his hands behind his yellow suspenders. "Might wait a day or two. Like to study it some," he said, his voice almost a murmur, turning away, finished with the conversation. Then suddenly he turned back. "Anyways, I want that horse!"

He spat reflectively. "'Course if I took 'em along,

they'd by God have to earn their bread. I ain't supportin' ne'er-do-wells. I surely ain't!"

And he walked away before Windy could reply—not that he had anything much to say to that.

The boy had, of course, not spoken. He had stopped whittling and was sitting crosslegged, studying the knife and the stick.

Windy had been watching him. "Whittling can do a man good," he said. "Helps you think. Good for the digestion. Gets the blood moving. Next best thing to girls," he concluded with a grin.

But the boy's face remained without expression. Now he held the stick in one hand and began slicing at it with the knife. It was a thick piece of wood, and Windy had already carved out several notches on it.

Suddenly a cry broke from the boy, and Windy saw the streak of red tracing along the back of his hand where the knife had slipped off the stick and cut him.

"Well, I'll be hornswaggled if you can't come out with *some* sound," the scout said, taking the knife and stick from him. "Here, let me take a look at her."

Slowly the boy moved his hand forward.

Windy frowned at the cut, his jaws working. "She'll do. Just hold your hand up for a spell, that'll help stop it. What bleeding's been done will wash it out, keep it clean. Though that barlow knife was clean as a nun's mind." He spat, then continued, speaking louder than usual, as though it would help the boy to hear better and maybe even respond. "See, the blood, it moves like a river, downstream always. So if you raise your arm like that, she'll have trouble moving upstream."

The boy did as he was told, still not uttering a word. They sat in silence for a while, and at length Windy stood up and started to walk away. He had it in mind to walk over to Tipi Town and socialize a bit and see what gossip he might pick up on the emigrant trains, but he'd only gone a few yards when he felt the boy behind him.

When he stopped and turned, he found the boy stopped too. He was still holding his hand up, though there was no more bleeding. "Come on," he said. "We'll go stroll out by the paddock. Don't figger Tipi Town's exactly the place for you, after what you been through."

Flora Conway, on the other hand, was having no trouble in getting Nellie to talk. At Conway's suggestion, she had taken the girl on as a sort of housemaid and helper, mostly for herself, but also for her mother.

"I've talked with both of them," Conway told his wife, "and so has Matt. But it's still not too clear."

"Well, I know the boy doesn't talk at all," Flora had said. "But what about the girl? Can't she give you some kind of a straight story?"

"She's all right. But there are just some points missing that she may have forgotten. I mean, what they went through must have been really rough. The fight in Nebraska, and this latest at Owl Creek."

"I can imagine. Well, we can give them time and care," Flora said.

"You know, Zachary is not actually her brother. She never laid eyes on him until she and her uncle left St. Joe with a wagon train bound for Oregon."

"What about her parents?" Flora asked. "Doesn't the child have parents?"

"Dear Flora, I do wish you would stop referring to that young lady as a child." Warner Conway's eyes twinkled into a smile as he looked fondly at his wife. "Why, she has every man on the post after her."

"Including the commanding officer?" And Flora's grin was wicked enough to break them both into laughter.

"Now, Flora, you watch that. You know who the commanding officer of Easy Company spends his time chasing."

Again she was serious. "I know, dear. Forgive me, but what about the girl's family?"

"Nellie and Zachary and apparently Ethan Deal, too— from what he's told Windy—were the sole survivors of a wagon train rubout. Probably Sioux—that's what Windy thinks. Deal and his wife were part of the train. His wife was killed, so he took Nellie and Zachary—or whatever his real name is—along with him. All I can say is, they were damn lucky!"

"But Nellie's parents," Flora said. "You say she was traveling with her uncle."

"That's what she told me. But it's where her story gets soft, if you know what I mean."

Flora shook her head. "Oh, God, it's so dreadful, Warner. I mean, when it happens to children." Flora realized she'd called Nellie a child again, but there was no objection this time from her husband.

"I guess that's what happened to Zachary; I mean, his parents or whoever he might have been traveling with were killed. And he's still not recovered from the shock. What I'm hoping is that if you could get to know one or both of them, it would be a help. Meanwhile, Regiment will try to locate any family. And when we can, we'll get the boy to a doctor."

"Of course I'll do all I can, dear." She hesitated and then said, "Deal. Deal is the strange one. There is something really peculiar about him."

"A self-styled man of God," Conway said. "I have the feeling now and again that he's a man of that other party, if you know who I mean."

Flora was frowning. "I do indeed. It's as though—I don't know—there is something dark about him, as I see it."

"Funny thing, my dear, that's exactly how I see Deal. As a color, too. Dark, as you say. Even black."

Subsequently, Flora found Nellie to be good company. The girl was bright, quick, and easy to get on with. She had an excellent figure. Her great attraction was her eyes, but also the way she moved. It was not that she was flirtatious; she was just lively, and she had an open friendliness, which, at the same time, revealed a quality of shyness that was singularly appealing. *Innocence* was the word that came to Flora's mind.

Mrs. Dodgson thought otherwise. "Hah! Indeed! Innocent as some of those I've seen in my time. Flora, you've always been a good girl. I brought you up that way—and at great cost, let me add, and despite your father, may his soul rest in peace. But mark you, that girl—well, I'm suspicious. You've seen the way the men look. You think she doesn't know it? The hussy!"

"Mother! She's just a child."

"Child! Have you seen that figure? And isn't she for showing her shape? That walk! You're the one who is innocent, Flora. Ever since you were a baby girl, that's been your main characteristic. Innocence. Lucky I saw you got the right husband. You don't know men, Flora. But you can take it from me, there's only one thing they're interested in, and you'd best know what that is. And that little hussy there, she knows it. Oh, she knows it!"

As it happened, Mrs. Dodgson was right, to a degree. Nellie was fully aware of the men's reaction to her as she crossed the parade. But it had been like that ever since she'd "developed," as her own mother had put it. Yes, they were all interested in only one thing. Her three brothers had been. Her dad had been. And so had Ethan Deal.

They were seated on the paddock fence, where the poles met at a corner, on the south side of Outpost Number Nine.

"Now then," Windy was saying, 'I'm gonna show

you how to whittle." Leaning on his knees, with his feet on the bar below him, he began to cut into the stick. "See, you can just whittle like nothin', just cutting wood, or you can cut out a figure—like a buffalo or a bird or something like that." He looked across at his small companion, who was listening intently with his cap pulled low on his head and with a hedge of white-blond hair sticking out all around the edges.

"First thing, of course," Windy continued, "is you got to have a real sharp blade, and clean. And you got to protect your fingers and hands. Got it?"

The boy's blue eyes were wide as he listened to Windy. He looked down at the scout's hands as they began to whittle the stick.

"See how easy it is? Maybe I'll cut out a small top. You watch me close, then you try it. You got it, Zack?" And he looked at the boy solemnly and lowered the lid over his left eye, keeping the other eye wide open, his face dead serious.

Windy wasn't absolutely certain, but he had a notion, just for the moment, that there was a change in the boy. He even wondered if there hadn't been a new light in those blue eyes. Then suddenly, as he watched, he saw those big blue eyes fill with tears, while the boy's lower lip began to quiver. But he didn't let out a sound.

"Let it out," Windy said. "Let it all out. That's what you be needing."

The boy struggled to hold back the tears, bending his head down behind the bill of his cap to watch Windy working with the barlow knife and the stick of wood. Not a sound. But, stealing a look at the side of his face, Windy saw the line of tears flowing down one cheek.

The sun was nearly at the horizon now, and the late, rich afternoon light fell across the sod-and-lumber buildings of the outpost.

"I'm hungry," Windy said. "You hungry, Zack?"

The boy didn't answer. From the nearby stable came the sound of nickering. A horse stamped, and the muffled curse of a soldier reached them.

The dying light was brilliant now, the sun sinking below the horizon. The boy and the man continued to sit there on the paddock fence, the man now and again talking, whittling with the last warmth of the sun on his hands and face. And the boy watching, saying nothing.

seven ———————————

The commanding officer of Easy Company was engaged in one of his most enjoyable pastimes. The new shipment of his favorite cigars had just arrived from San Francisco, and now, seated with Matt Kincaid and Windy Mandalian in his office, he was engrossed in opening his package.

"I hope you gentlemen realize what an auspicious moment this is," he was saying, his large face wreathed in a joyous smile.

"I personally am right with you, sir," Matt said, grinning from his seat on the other side of the room.

"They'll never make one of them see-gars good enough for chawing," Windy said, peeling himself a sizable portion from his big slab of cut-plug. "Though I will allow, if a man does have to smoke, those stogies of the captain's is the next best thing to a tasty chaw."

"Does that heavy-handed hint mean that you would like one?" Conway said, removing the last wrapping from the box and gazing on his prize.

"Nope." Windy popped his fresh chew into his mouth, and began working it slowly.

Silence fell while the two officers lighted their cigars and indulged in the first luxurious puff.

"Gentlemen, let us get down to business." Conway put his cigar down in the ashtray at his elbow and, leaning forward, laced his fingers together.

Matt uncrossed his legs while Windy, over by the window, squatted on his haunches and pushed the brim of his hat upward with his forefinger so that he could see better.

"Well, sir," Matt said, "it appears we're turning into the Wyoming Prairie Hotel." And he added quickly, "I'm not including Mrs. Dodgson in that remark."

Conway chuckled. "It does feel that way. Sure, we've had all kinds of visitors before, but this bunch seems pretty unique. Matt, I know you weren't referring to Mrs. D., but I am. We're all of age, and I know you can see that while Mavis is a lovely woman in a great many ways—I am actually very fond of her—she is at the same time driving our honorable mess sergeant into screaming nightmares. Not to mention, now and again, your commanding officer."

Windy sniffed. "She is a lady who knows everything," he said. "I locked horns with her. She started tellin' me all about the Sioux and Cheyenne, then told me I oughta get married and raise a family."

"Be careful," Conway said, with a wink at Kincaid. "Next thing you know, she'll be telling you how to chew tobacco."

Windy had been sitting on his heels, hunched into his shoulders, and now suddenly he whipped his head straight up to the top of his long neck, like a turkey, blinking his eyes and wagging his head. "You think she ain't done worse than that already, by God, instructing yours truly on where to spit!"

At that point both Conway and Kincaid collapsed into raucous laughter, while Windy scowled at them and chewed more vigorously than ever.

"I must say that my mother-in-law is indeed into everything on this outpost. She has even instructed Ben Cohen on how to run the company."

"Who won?" Matt asked."

"Let me say that Ben—God bless him—didn't lose. Mrs. D. informed our first sergeant that the men smelled vile and should bathe—not more frequently, but 'less infrequently'! You can imagine how that fine line went over with Ben Cohen."

"Well," said Matt. "I know she told Dutch Rothausen if his cooking tasted as bad as it smelled, the men would be down with diarrhea and maybe even cholera within a week."

The laughter had left Warner Conway's face. "You know, we joke about it, but something's got to be done. Mavis Dodgson is a menace. *I mean she is into everything!*" Conway dropped his hand helplessly onto his desk. His bleak eyes looked at Windy and Matt. He had forgotten his cigar. "I need your help. And as much as I hate to tell you this, she could be here for a while." He spread his hands helplessly. "What can I do? Just what the hell can I do?"

An appalling silence fell in the room at those words. Matt stared at a spider walking across the ceiling. Windy's chewing slowed perceptibly.

At last it was the scout who came up with an interesting suggestion. "Got me a idea."

Both heads turned eagerly in his direction.

63

" 'Course, it might put some hackles up, and I don't mean no offense. Still, you did ask." He was looking at Conway.

"Never mind all that palaver," the captain said. "Get to the point. What the hell can we do to stop her meddling? I mean, she wants to go for a walk outside the perimeter every afternoon. I've got to assign two men to go along with her, and you know how undermanned we are already!"

"The lady needs herself a husband," Windy said.

There was no reaction from either of the two officers. The statement was a simple, obvious solution. Awesome, most probably unattainable, yet remorseless.

Presently Windy detached himself from the frozen tableau, rising and crossing to the spittoon beside Conway's desk, into which he spat a thick stream of tobacco juice. Returning to his squatting position by the window, he looked down at the floor between his legs. Then he looked up at the ceiling, but feeling something different in the room, he turned his attention to Conway and Kincaid, both of whom had their gaze leveled at him.

The silence grew longer. Neither Conway nor Kincaid took their eyes away from the scout.

"Now just wait a minute!" Windy suddenly found his tongue, holding his hands as though to stop the thought that he could see they were thinking. "Just a minute. I may be a doctor, but I sure as hell ain't the medicine. By God, you stop that!" His voice rose and he stood up while Conway and Matt broke into loud laughter. But to Windy Mandalian there was nothing funny in the situation.

The laughter was so loud that First Sergeant Ben Cohen, seated at his desk outside in the orderly room, raised his head in wonder. Were they going loopy in there? He shrugged. Could be. It could be, he told himself.

Inside Conway's office, order and calm were finally restored.

"The other problem," Conway was saying, "is what to do with Ethan Deal and those two young ones. I can call in Regiment, who will handle the situation in their usual efficient manner."

"You mean bounce it back on us," Matt said.

"Exactly."

"What's the alternative, sir? Deal can handle himself. But I'd hate to see Nellie and the boy get shifted all over the place."

"Flora has become friends with Nellie," Conway said. "The girl turns out to be educated, and generally a nice sort. Both Flora and I are fond of her. She draws pretty much a blank on the wagon train raid. Which isn't surprising, after all." Conway stretched his arm out on the desk, looking at the backs of his fingers. "She could be sent on to her family in Oregon, only she doesn't know where they are. Her uncle must have known, but of course he's dead."

"How old is she?" Windy asked.

"Says she's nineteen, and I believe her," Matt said. "I had a long talk with her, amounting to about the same as you've said, sir."

"The girl is smart," Conway said. "Maybe she could end up teaching school someplace." He spread his hands. "It would be a pity if she got off on the wrong foot, is how Flora has put it. And I do agree."

"And the boy?" Matt asked.

"He's a corker." Windy scratched his chest and then the back of his left arm. He moved his tobacco to the front of his mouth now, his lips pursing a little. Conway was watching the ruminative way the scout moved his jaws. He had never known Windy to move fast, except when it was absolutely necessary, and then he was light-

65

ning. He missed nothing. Like an Indian, Conway thought. Maybe there was truth in the story that he had Cree blood.

"He still doesn't speak?" Matt asked.

"Not around me, leastways."

"You'd know if he did," observed Conway. "You've got that kid for a shadow."

"Teaching him sign language," Windy said. "He's picking it up real fast." He paused. Then he resumed, "Kid's scared shitless. Thought it might help him to work some chores around the post. Providing that's all right with the commanding officer, the adjutant, and—uh"— he threw his thumb toward the orderly room—"the Sarge out there."

"Damn good idea," Conway said. "You agree, Matt?"

"Yes, sir. I can speak to Ben about it."

"He needs people," Windy said, and scratched the inside of his thigh.

"Good," Conway said. "Well, we've got a few around here. Meanwhile, I have informed Regiment of their presence on the post." He paused, looking across at the wall map. "Now then, what about Deal?"

"I told him Faraway Eagle's proposition, sir." A wry grin broke over Matt's face. "He as much as told me I was crazy. He said he insisted on the Cheyennes giving him the horse, and that's all there was to talk about."

"You know he don't have a chance in a knife fight with one of them Contraries." Windy said.

"I certainly agree," said Matt. "But we have to come up with something."

"We do have until the end of the month, however," Conway pointed out. "I know that isn't long, but right now I'm concerned about the youngsters." He paused.

"Of course, Deal is free to go wherever and whenever he likes," Conway went on. "I've spoken to him about assuming some responsibility for those two youngsters, since he did bring them this far. But I don't think it made much of an impression. He just keeps saying he wants the army to get him his horse. What do you think, Matt?"

"I'd give him another day or two, sir, and then brace him. He looks to me like he's got something pretty heavy on his mind. I mean, he was like that at the beginning, and it seems even worse now."

The figure by the window stirred. "If you want my opinion—and I am sure you do not—it is as follows: I wouldn't feel any too happy about anybody—man, woman, child, or beast—in that gentleman's company. He is plumb crazy." And Windy clamped his jaws shut.

Whatever Warner Conway started to say in reply to that was cut off by the knock at the door.

It was Ben Cohen. "Sir, Mr. Deal requests some time with you. I wouldn't have interrupted you," Cohen continued, lowering his voice and stepping farther into the room, "except he looks kind of strange."

"Strange?"

"He looks kind of wild, Captain."

"Is he out there?" Conway looked at Matt, his eyebrows raised.

"Yes, sir. I can have him wait. But I didn't know how important it was, and he won't say what his business is. I mean, sir, he looks a little like he's gone round the bend."

"I understand, Sergeant." Conway turned back to Matt and Windy. "I think we can all hear what Mr. Deal has to say. Send him in, Sergeant."

The man who entered the captain's office was certainly distraught. Where before his face and general mien had been somber, it was now as though some agony twisted inside him. Matt Kincaid wondered for a moment if the man was mad.

"Sit down, Mr. Deal," Conway said, indicating a chair.

67

"Is what you wish to speak about something private, or may my adjutant and chief scout be present? It's entirely up to you, sir."

The long, leathery face turned toward Kincaid and Windy. Ethan Deal said nothing.

"Sit down, sir," Conway said again. "I haven't spoken with you since your experience with the Cheyenne Contraries, though I've certainly been meaning to."

Deal sat hunched in his chair. Now he tried to straighten his shoulders, but could not, though he did manage to sit slightly more erect. The man looked as though he had been crushed by some great weight, or was it an illness?

"Captain Conway, I got something to tell you."

"Have you decided something about Nellie and Zachary, is that it?"

Those burning eyes, so deep in their sockets, looked directly at Conway now, and it was all the captain could do not to look away.

"Captain, I be a man of the Lord, and I have done evil. I have committed the ultimate sin. I have told God, and now I must tell man."

"What is it, Mr. Deal?" Conway felt something pull at him, something he didn't like but could not name.

Suddenly Deal reached up and took off his hat. He held it with both hands in front of him. Now he raised his head, his wide, bony shoulders still bowed and twisted, his dry lips moving as though in prayer, or perhaps in rehearsal of what he wanted to say.

"I ask the forgiveness of the Lord, Captain Conway, and of man. I am a heartless, miserable sinner." His eyes dropped to the floor and he was again cloaked in silence.

"Mr. Deal, won't you—" Conway began, but something in the look Deal turned upon him now stopped him.

"Captain Conway, I got to tell somebody. I've already told the Lord."

"What, Mr. Deal? What do you want to tell?"

The lips started to move, but for a moment no sound came. Then they all heard it, soft yet clear, as though it came from the four walls of the room.

"I killed my wife. I killed her at the Indian attack on the wagon train. I murdered Hester..."

eight ─────────────

Ethan Deal's words seemed to echo in Conway's office, challenging the charged silence that enveloped Conway, Kincaid, and Windy Mandalian as they looked in shock at the New Englander.

Conway was the first to break the silence. "You say you murdered your wife, Deal? You killed her?"

Ethan Deal sat bent over, his shoulders more twisted than ever it seemed. "That is so. I killed Hester." The man's eyes stared far beyond the room.

"Was it an accident?"

"No, I murdered her."

"Why?" asked Kincaid. "Can I ask you why, sir? Did you have an argument, a fight with her?"

Ethan Deal's big head shook under his big black hat. "I just killed her," he said, and he drew in his breath as though not wanting to let go of it. "I hated her."

"How?" Windy asked. He was squatting by the window and his eyes squinted across the room at Deal. "How did you kill her?"

"Hit her over the head with a rifle barrel. It was lying there right next to me in the wagon when I come to. I just picked it up and..."

Conway looked at him, perplexed. Deal spoke without any expression whatever in his voice. Conway had heard that voice before, from survivors of hostile attacks. It was as though the horror had been driven deep into the person, to a place where there was no longer any feeling. And the slightest release—even a trickle—would set off an avalanche of pain too unendurable to accommodate.

"This happened at Scott's Wells?" Conway asked. "I just want to get my facts straight."

"During the raid," Deal said, speaking to the far corner of the room. "The one where I found the boy and girl."

Conway reached behind him to the table, where he kept some glasses, and now he opened the little cupboard at the bottom of his desk and took out the bottle of brandy.

"You'd better have this," he said, passing it to Matt, who had risen.

Deal looked at the dark brown fluid Matt handed him and downed it at a gulp.

"It was after the raid. Like I told you, I got knocked out. When I come to, there was nobody around, just Hester lying there." He paused, his mouth working, forming special words. "I seen she was alive. There was this rifle right there next to me. I picked it up and..." His eyes stared, he raised his hand, the fingers bent like a claw. "And..." His whole body shook and he let the hand fall as all his breath seemed to escape him.

"Then what happened?" Conway asked.

"Then?" He seemed to pull himself back into the room. "Then I come upon the two youngsters. They come out of hiding when them red heathens took off, I guess. They was standing there, and I found my two mules—guess

72

they only wanted hosses—and we left. We didn't bury nobody, we just left. We didn't even bury Hester. We was afraid. Oh, we was fierce afraid!"

"You didn't run into an army patrol or anyone?" Matt asked, looking at the man carefully.

"Run into nobody, thank the Lord. Only when we met them crazy contrastings or whatever you call 'em. Then...then we come here." He raised his eyes to the ceiling. "Praise God I found the courage to confess my terrible deed."

"What kind of a rifle did you hit your wife with?" The question came from the corner of the room by the window, where Windy Mandalian was squatting. Both Conway and Kincaid looked at the scout.

"What does that matter?" Deal asked. "I dunno what kind of gun it was." He seemed angry for a moment and then he said, "Yes, I recollect it. It was my own Henry."

Conway was leaning back away from his desk, his hands on the edge of the wooden top, his eyes measuring Ethan Deal. "How do you feel, Mr. Deal?" he asked suddenly, and he threw a glance to Matt Kincaid.

"Could use another," he said. And Conway poured generously.

"I suggest that you could be mistaken about what happened," Conway said slowly, with his eyes directly on Deal.

The belligerence was back in a flash. "How so? You don't believe what I am saying?"

"Oh, I believe it," Conway said swiftly. He looked toward his adjutant. "Don't you, Matt?"

"I do, sir. But I also believe Mr. Deal is mistaken. I think we are both saying"—and he glanced at Windy—"in fact, we're all three saying that Mr. Deal did not kill his wife. But he thinks he did."

Kincaid had his eyes on Deal as he spoke. The New Englander continued to stare straight across the room, but now his lips pursed and he frowned as he dropped his eyes to the floor. "I told you I killed Hester. That is the way of it. I am telling you the God's truth."

Conway leaned forward. "Mr. Deal, none of us doubts your word. What we are saying is that from the evidence you have given us, it isn't likely you did kill you wife, but that when you came to after being knocked out, you found her dead and blamed yourself for not having defended her, blamed yourself that you had survived and she hadn't. This is not uncommon, sir."

"What the hell evidence you talkin' about, Captain!"

"No Indians ever leave weapons lying around after a raid. They need all the guns they can get. Your Henry wouldn't have been left there, you can be sure of that. Sir, I am going to ask the regimental doctor to have a look at you, but I'm pretty certain his view will support what these two gentlemen and I have to say."

In the pause that followed, Deal's big body began to shake, and then he was sobbing.

The two officers and the scout waited. There was nothing else to do. Ethan Deal continued to sob, his great shoulders shaking. He was sweating all through his thick head of hair.

All of them watched as he turned his tortured face heavenward. "Oh, Hester, forgive me. Dear God, forgive me . . ."

He continued to sob and shake. It was as though his body were being beaten. But there was something missing, as the other three saw. There were no tears coming out of his eyes.

Presently Conway poured brandy for all of them.

In the captain's office the silence lengthened. Ethan Deal's confession had exhausted them all.

nine _____

"Why, what do you mean it takes four minutes to boil a three-minute egg? I never heard of such a thing!"

Mavis Dodgson stood, arms akimbo, in the center of the kitchen, her dark eyes fixed on Dutch Rothausen, whose great hulk almost filled the entire space between the kitchen range and the big table in the center of the room.

"Ma'am," Dutch explained with excruciating patience, "it ain't myself decided it. It's the way it is. It's something to do with the altitude."

"Attitude! What do you mean attitude? Whose attitude?"

"I said *al*titude! roared Dutch. "We're very high up, here."

"Oh, then why didn't you say so? I know we're high up. My son-in-law tells me that is why I've been getting so out of breath."

She paused, her eyes darting about. "I think the place

looks halfway decent now. I'm sure you agree, Sergeant."

Dolefully, Dutch surveyed the changes she had wrought in his kitchen. For two days Mavis Dodgson had been cleaning and rearranging. He had bent to her wishes; after all, she was the captain's mother-in-law, and Conway had asked him to go along as much as he could. It was just unfair as hell that she had picked the kitchen and mess hall for her attack. Why not the orderly room? Sure, she'd invaded Ben Cohen's domain, but only to a limited extent, nothing like she'd done in the kitchen and mess hall. Dutch was no longer so sure that peace was better than outright warfare.

Suddenly a smile broke across Mavis Dodgson's face. Dutch was startled, and instantly suspicious. What was she up to now?

"Sergeant Rothausen, I appreciate your indulging an elderly lady. But you know, I'm of Swiss and English ancestry, and I just cannot stand filth and disorder; especially in a kitchen." She paused; the smile had not completely left her face, and now her eyes brightened as she said, "I would dearly love a cup of your excellent coffee."

Dutch wasn't sure how to take it, so he simply nodded. After two long days of nagging, aggressive suggestion, he was thrown by the sudden change.

"Sure," he said.

"You'll join me, won't you?"

Dutch nodded. He didn't want any more coffee, but he was too surprised by her change in tactics to say no.

She beamed on him as he sat down across from her with the two steaming mugs of coffee. "You know, Sergeant Rothausen, it's the strange conditions you people live in out here that strike me. The dirt! Why, during that rainstorm the other night, all the muddy water leaked into my room. Then, when it isn't raining, the walls shed straw dust. And those earth floors! All the furniture gets covered with dust, and it's in the food too. Why, there's actually grit in your teeth when you eat sometimes!"

"That I know, ma'am. But on the other hand, those rammed-earth walls and roofs keep us safe from bullets and fire arrows. It's a real strong fortress. And it's cheap, built from the materials at hand."

Mavis Dodgson's large bosom heaved in a copious sigh. Yes, it was what Warner had told her. And Flora. And the other big, red-faced sergeant—what was his name? Anyhow, they all had reasons for everything. There just seemed such a lack of efficiency around the post. She had addressed herself to whatever came within her purview—the kitchen and mess, the stables, the orderly room, the men's barracks. She had driven Ben Cohen into a barely controlled fury by suggesting that the men clean their fingernails. Oh, she knew how she affected all of them, including Warner Conway, but it was necessary. Efficiency was the mainstay of a sensible life. Men were such fools!

She let her gaze fall upon Dutch Rothausen, noting the bulging eyes—like a couple of painted eggs, she reflected. "Now, Sergeant, I've a good suggestion for your breakfast tomorrow. Would you have any objection to my helping you plan something tasteful and good for the men?"

Dutch, relaxing at last in the warmth of what had appeared to be a cessation of interference, was suddenly whipped into alarm and anger at himself for being caught off guard once again.

He turned white, his great, red-rimmed eyes pointed upward. "The meal has already been planned, Mrs. Dodgson." But he knew it was already a losing battle. It was dreadful, he told himself, what a man had to go through in this army. And for the very first time in his career at Outpost Number Nine he found himself wishing that Ben Cohen, the redoubtable first sergeant, was beside him. He had not even had such a wish during the times hostile Indians had attacked Number Nine. But then, of course, it had been simple; he had known what to do. Here, under the gimlet-eyed mother-in-law of his commanding officer, he was at a total loss.

Yet the man from whom Dutch had imaginatively sought succor was presently standing in front of Captain Conway's desk with the question that was rapidly sweeping through Easy Company. "Sir, might I ask—for clarity—just how far you wish me to go in allowing Mrs. Dodgson to, uh..." He paused, searching for the right word.

"To butt into your business, Sergeant?"

"Yes, sir. Exactly that, sir. Not that she isn't a very nice lady, Captain. But she, uh, does show an extra amount of interest in things that my office usually keeps private."

Warner Conway controlled the smile that started at the corners of his mouth; his face was bland as he looked at his first sergeant. "Ben, you should go have a talk with Dutch Rothausen. You've got it easy."

"Captain, I've been listening to Rothausen. I know I haven't had as much interference as he has, but my office is a more sensitive area."

"True," Conway agreed. "True. We do have to keep to our organizational procedures. No question. I'll have a talk with Mrs. Dodgson."

"Thank you, sir."

As the door closed behind Cohen, Conway looked across at Matt Kincaid, who was surveying him rather grimly.

"You, Matt? Have you been favored with Mrs. Dodgson's attentions?"

"No, sir. Or I should say, perhaps—and with all due respect, sir—not yet."

"Wait." Conway shook his head wearily. "The woman is indefatigable. She never sleeps. She's after Flora to redecorate. She wants to build Flora and me a special cabin out of wood so the rooms will be clean. She's told Ben Cohen the men smell, she's told Rothausen there's no variety in his food. She doesn't approve of the way Reb McBride blows reveille."

"Yes, sir. Reb's trumpet was a bit nervous-sounding this morning."

"Matt, we're old friends, besides being comrades-in-arms. So let's cut the 'with all due respect' bullshit. The woman is a pain in the ass, let's face it. The question is, what can be done to contain her?"

"The latest," Flora Conway was saying to her husband, 'is that mother is concerned about Nellie."

"I think we're all concerned about Nellie and Zachary," Conway said, feeling the lurch in his stomach, a tightening that seemed to increase each time he heard something new about Mavis Dodgson.

"No, I don't mean that," Flora said.

"What do you mean, then?"

"I'm talking about her being a young girl amid a lot of hungry men."

"Are you serious, Flora?"

"Mother is. She objects to the way some of the men look at Nellie."

They were sitting in their front room, having their evening drink, waiting for Mavis to appear for dinner.

"You know, Warner, Nellie is a very pretty young lady, and you must have noticed that she isn't shaped exactly like a stick of wood."

"Flora, are you suggesting that that young girl is encouraging the men?"

"What I am saying is, she doesn't have to."

At this point there came a determined knock at the

door, and almost before Flora could answer, it opened and in walked her mother.

"Ah, time for a drink. Good. I'd been looking so forward to it."

Conway was already pouring. "Here you are."

Without a moment's hesitation, her hand flowing toward the glass of whiskey to take it from her son-in-law's custody, Mavis Dodgson expertly brought the drink to her lips.

"Ah, that's a bit of all right after a long day, I must say! This dry air, it absolutely cracks my lips. And my hair—I can't do a thing with it, it's like wire!"

Flora smiled fondly at her mother and sipped her drink, while Warner Conway retreated into his chair, thinking of the good cigar he was going to have after dinner.

"Do you know, I shouldn't say this to either of you, only I will. I will. Do you know, that big mess sergeant, I do believe he has his eye on me."

"Mother!"

"Now don't be shocked, Flora. You know, Warner, how perfectly staid and *proper* Flora is! I've tried to bring her up to be more aware of . . . well, of what's going on in the world, but she is *prim*. I've always said so!"

Conway had great difficulty in keeping his face straight. "But she has other good qualities, Mavis," he said gently, swiftly sneaking a look at his wife's buttocks as she rose to check their supper.

"But of course!" Mrs. Dodgson dropped her eyes swiftly to her own bosom and reached for her glass. Little lines appeared at the corners of her eyes as she smiled. "I know I am getting on, as the saying goes, but this fort or post, or whatever it's called, is absolutely full of men. And we all know what men are. No offense, Warner, dear, but it's the way of the world. As I have said again and again, I've always tried to bring this realization to my only child." And she turned to Flora as she came back into the room, all but squirming under her mother's fond gaze.

"Mother, there are other things besides men in the world."

"That's what you always say, my dear child." Her mouth suddenly formed into a sort of secret smile as her eyes lighted with recollection. "You know, I do find your Sergeant Cone rather cute."

"Holy Mother of God!" Conway roared suddenly, almost dropping his drink, and both he and Flora dissolved in laughter.

"Good heavens, what did I say!"

"Cute!" roared Conway. "Wait'll I tell that to Maggie Cohen!"

"Mother, the name is Cohen, not Cone."

"Is it, dear? But why are you both laughing so? Perhaps you don't see what a little boy he is at heart; and I must say, he's not at all bad-looking." She sniffed and, drawing out her handkerchief, dabbed at her nose. "But you're not going to tell this person Maggie—I presume she's his wife—oh, yes, I did meet her."

"That is what she is," Conway said, dabbing the tears from his eyes. He sighed. "Mavis, let me tell you, it's great having you here." And he meant it—knowing, too, that he was going to regret the remark pretty soon.

"But Warner, you mustn't say anything of the kind about the poor man to his wretched wife. The poor woman would be after me with a gun, or a meat cleaver, more likely, judging by the shape of her figure. I know those Irish washerwoman types! Now, Warner Conway, I spoke in confidence to you. After all, I can't feel free to report to you on the condition of things if what I say isn't held in the strictest confidence."

"Mother, don't worry about it. Besides, I'm sure that Maggie Cohen thinks Ben is just as cute as you think he is." As she said this, Flora had a terrible time keeping her face straight. The result was that she looked rather furiously at her mother.

But, as Warner Conway had long noted, Mavis Dodgson was impervious to many of the nuances of life, and he decided that in the long run this was probably just as well.

"But it's actually that young girl, Nellie, I am concerned with," Mavis continued, her eyebrows shooting up toward her hairline and her eyes popping out at her daughter and son-in-law, who simply looked away, trying not to look at each other.

Realizing that Mrs. Dodgson was only pausing in order to sip at her drink and would then rush on, Warner Conway seized the moment to speak. "Mavis," he said in a pleasantly chiding tone, "you're speaking of the American military man, so please show due respect." And he beamed on his mother-in-law, thinking wryly, *God, I'd hate to have to fight a campaign with her on the other side.*

Mrs. Dodgson bent toward her host, her lips pressed together, her chin slightly puckered. Then, with humor in her eyes, she said, "I respect all of them, even that Irishman who never stops talking, that big one. Maloney."

"Malone."

"Whatever. The one with the wandering eyes, the musical tongue. I was in the kitchen, working with the sergeant of the mess—and let me tell you, Warner Conway, something has got to be done about the food! I can see why you call it 'mess'; that's just what it is. Not that Sergeant Ruthouse doesn't make a fair cup of coffee. Anyway, that Irish *person* had his eye on me. No question! Those big Irish eyes. Why, I could feel it almost the whole time I was there." She sighed, bringing her fingertips to her bosom. "Warner, dear man, do freshen my glass. You know, my doctor—you remember Dr. Fenimore Agrippa, don't you, Flora?—he's always insisted that a drop of the demon rum, as my late husband called it, was the best medicine for what*ever* ails you. In my case, of course, it's helped my hearing."

"I have always known you to have the best hearing of anyone I've ever met, Mother," Flora said, her eyes turning in exasperation to Warner Conway.

"But of course!"

And Flora found, as she always had, that her mother's smugness in the face of challenge infuriated her.

Mrs. Dodgson tapped the glass of brown liquid. "Because of this, my dear." She paused, looking at their two glasses, which Warner had also refilled. "But taken in good measure." She raised her index finger to emphasize her point. "Taken in good measure."

Flora had risen and gone out to see how the dinner was. "Everything's ready," she called from the next room. "We can start."

"Oh!" Mavis looked startled. "Isn't that nice young lieutenant coming for dinner? I so enjoyed his company last time."

"Not tonight, Mother. We thought that tonight just the three of us could enjoy each other's conversation. It makes a nice change."

Mrs. Dodgson had risen. 'Why do you suppose he's not married?"

"Who?"

"Lieutenant Fincaid. The person I was just speaking about!"

"It's Kincaid, with a K."

"Whatever it is, I still have my question. Why isn't he married? He's certainly one of the most attract—"

"He's still a young man," Flora cut in, fighting weariness in the face of her mother's barrage. "And besides, women don't grow on trees out here."

"Well, I know his type. He's full of fun and frolic, that one. Oh, yes." She smiled at the ceiling. "One can always tell the bird by its flight!"

They had seated themselves now, and Flora looked across at her mother. "Mother, you cannot get me to believe that Matt Kincaid, who is young enough to be your son—and please excuse me—was ogling you, as you like to put it!"

"And why not, my dear child?" Mavis Dodgson raised her head so that the tip of her nose pointed directly at her daughter. Then, perhaps satisfied at having hit her target, she looked down at her hands as she spread them along the edge of the table before her. "He could do worse."

ten ———————

The two figures lying in the twilight looked like one. They were just beyond the perimeter line outside Outpost Number Nine, in a small copse of trees, protected from the view of anyone passing by on the trail toward regimental headquarters, or walking the parapet of the outpost.

Nellie was lying on her back, with her legs wrapped around the waist of Private Harvey Barker. The young man was heavy on her, and she kept trying to move her position to get rid of a sharp object that was sticking into her left kidney, but she didn't want to interrupt their shared pleasure. And so, as her body undulated with joy, she tried to shift her weight away from the object sticking into her back. But now, at a sudden burst of almost maniacal passion from her partner, Nellie forgot completely about the branch, or whatever it was, and devoted herself wholly to the consummation of her desire.

"By heck, that's the best piece I ever," said the young man as his hips slowed in their bucking motion.

"Glad to hear that," Nellie said, her breathing returning to normal. "Wasn't sure you was getting what you wanted."

"Got that and more," he said, breathing into her hair.

"Think it beats soldierin', do you?" she asked, and bit his earlobe.

"Ouch!"

"Hurt you?"

"No."

"Then why'd you yell?"

"'Cause I liked it."

She wiggled beneath him and stuck her tongue in his mouth.

"Better stop that."

"Why?"

"You'll be gettin' more."

"I'm not complaining." She could feel his member growing again inside her, and she began to move her hips slowly.

"Oh, my God," he muttered. "You got me coming again."

Nellie, however, was speechless as they rode each other to an ecstatic climax, and then lay gasping as their bodies subsided.

Suddenly Barker raised his head.

"What's the matter?"

"You hear something?"

"No. What?" She slipped her hands down his back to stroke his bare buttocks. "Want some more?"

"Jesus," said Harvey Barker. He raised up a little higher, listening. "I heard something. I know I did."

"I don't hear a thing."

"That's all I need, for the Sarge or somebody to find me out here like this." He drew himself out of her, looking around as he raised himself up on his hands and knees.

There was still some light, but the sun was clearly low on the horizon, though they could not see it. In the stand of trees, it was almost dark, with that slow changing in the air heralding the coming of the cool night.

He had risen and was pulling up his trousers, which he had never completely removed, and was now buttoning himself hurriedly. "You sure you didn't hear somethin?"

"Nothing. I didn't hear anything. Only the animals and . . . us."

"You sure?" There was the edge of fear in his voice.

"Come on. It was probably some animal."

"Yeah—sure." But he was only partly mollified as he tucked in his shirt and tightened his belt.

"Want to kiss me goodbye?" Nellie said as she raised herself up on her elbows, and then instantly wished she hadn't said it.

"I better get back to camp."

"You better."

Swift as a whistle he was gone, and it was darker.

Nellie continued to lie just where she was, looking up through the whispering branches to the darkening sky above. She didn't feel like moving. There was no place she wanted to go, especially, and she was not uncomfortable. She lay there thinking about Freddie, the little dog she'd had when she was a child back in Marysville, Ohio. She often wondered why she'd had a dog, why that had been allowed. It seemed that for some reason neither of them had much noticed the presence of Freddie, who always had the good sense—unlike herself—to stay out of their way. But one day the little dog had been slow in moving away and her father had kicked him, kicked him halfway across the yard. And the next thing Nellie knew, she had charged Olin Beko, beating at him with her little fists while Freddie lay squealing and broken in the dirt yard. Her father had knocked her flat with one stiff backhand and later, drunk as he was most every night, had beaten her mother, who, in turn, had hit Nellie across both ears and then taken a stick to her bare buttocks. When Freddie died the next day, Nellie buried him, then shook the dust of Marysville and went to visit her aunt in Columbus, who promptly put her into an orphanage. It was after escaping the orphanage that she met Clyde, a teamster who seduced her, and it was with him—as her "uncle"—that she was traveling to Oregon when the Indians attacked. One of them had raped her after killing Clyde, and then had thrown her into a big clump of bushes, indicating to her that he would come back. But he didn't. And so she had left the scene with Deal and the boy.

She lay there now in the copse, wishing she had some licorice to suck on.

Presently she heard a rustling only a few feet away, and then the sharp cracking of a branch.

"You can come out now," she said. "He won't be back."

She still didn't move as the steps came closer and the tall figure formed itself in the dark just above her.

"Thought you might like a little more."

"I don't mind."

"The soldier boy give you some money?"

"No."

"Goddammit, I told you!"

"I don't want to do that. I told you!"

"You better learn, Goddammit."

"No," she said. "I won't. Not for money."

"Shut your mouth," the man said as he opened his trousers.

Nellie didn't say anything. When Ethan Deal entered her she was thinking of Freddie, the little dog she'd buried very carefully along the stream that ran through the town dump back in Marysville.

In the hot forenoon the wagon train moved slowly across the dry plain. The party was weary, the horses flecked with dust and sweat; the half-dozen wagons were strung far apart, like a lazy snake under the heated blue sky. Yet the spirit of the emigrants was good, euphoric with the promise of the new land ahead—Oregon—and the far edge of the great continent. A new beginning, a new life.

It was around noon when the train approached the thick stand of cottonwood trees that ran along the bank of the creek.

"We'll go easy for a spell," said the tall wagonmaster. "Though we'll still keep peeled for hostiles like we been warned."

The two men riding with him at the head of the train nodded. The news they'd heard back at Scott's Wells of the Sioux massacre was still fresh in their thoughts.

"Looks pretty clear to me," said one of the three, a man named Soames.

Tyrone McCone, the wagonmaster, turned briskly in his stock saddle. "Can't be too careful, Clyde." His eyes studied the trees ahead.

"But this here ain't Sioux country, according to that old trapper at Beaver Crossing," said the third rider. "I know we got to be careful," he added quickly, seeing the look in McCone's face. "Just that I've heard the Cheyenne are friendlies."

"Don't matter what tribe they are, if they're on the warpath," McCone said, looking hard from under his heavy black eyebrows.

"Shit, I thought the army was supposed to protect us," Soames said.

"Army can't be everywhere," McCone pointed out,

then gazed forward and nodded. "That's Tiverton signaling up ahead," he said. "All clear. So we'll pull up just this side of the creek. Give the horses a blow, and the rest of us a rest."

They had just kneed their horses to push on when Tyrone McCone's right hand suddenly slapped to the holster at his waist.

A lone rider had suddenly appeared out of the trees without any warning. McCone raised his left hand while his right stayed on the gun butt, and the caravan came to a halt.

The stranger stood in his stirrups as he rode forward. He was a stocky man, dressed in buckskins, with a lot of long black curly hair upon which he wore a derby hat with a few holes in it. He was a handsome fellow, young, and he showed a lot of teeth in a broad smile as he reined his dappled pony and greeted McCone and the two other men at the head of the wagon train.

The wagonmaster returned the greeting, though guardedly. His eyes studied the stranger, while Soames and the third man, whose name was Delehanty, watched the trees ahead.

"Said hello to your point rider up there," the stranger said. "Name's Porter. I'm scouting for the U.S. Army. My patrol is back a piece. You'll be meeting up with 'em. They'll escort you a ways."

Smiles of relief broke on the faces of the three men.

"Tyrone McCone. This here is Clyde Soames and Fred Delehanty."

Porter touched the brim of his derby hat with his forefinger. "It's a hot one," he said.

"It is that," agreed McCone.

"You boys look like you've come a piece."

"All the way from Shaver's Station."

"Heading for the Bozeman?"

"And Oregon."

The scout's face spread into a big grin. "Got you a ways to go yet. But you'll make it good," he said. "Better bunch 'em up. Not that there's hostiles about; there ain't, and you got the army right with you in your pants pocket. Still, it's good to get in the habit of things." He grinned.

"Obliged, mister," said McCone. Turning in his saddle, he signaled with his arm for the wagons to move closer together.

Porter dropped his eyes to McCone's saddle boot. "See you got Henrys."

"Sure have. We all got 'em."

"It's a good weapon," Porter said.

"We'll be looking for game up ahead," Soames said.

The scout nodded. "Just passed a small herd of elk the other side of the creek. A buck and seven does. Ought to suit you right fine."

"Not much left of the buffalo, eh?"

"No, not much. Pretty well shot out. But there is plenty pronghorn and elk, and when you get to the mountains, there is sheep."

"Sheep?"

"Bighorns. Wild sheep. You'll need marksmen for them. They don't allow a man to get close."

"Like to offer you some hospitality," McCone said, keeping his horse closer.

"Obliged. But I better get riding. I got the army on my back." Porter laughed. "Got to earn my pay." Touching the brim of his hat again, he started along the trail.

"Friendly feller," Delehanty said as they watched the scout riding down the length of the wagon train, greeting the drivers along his way.

"We'll just pull up a few feet here," McCone said. "We don't need to worry now, with the army here." And as he spoke, a dozen mounted soldiers broke out of the trees.

The uniformed figure leading the patrol brought them

in at a trot. He was a big man with a long beard. Raising his left hand, he brought the patrol to a halt behind him. "Major Jellicoe at your service, sir!"

Porter Jellicoe had just reached the end of the wagon train and was exchanging pleasantries with the two riders bringing up the rear. He was, in fact, telling them a lively story he'd heard in a Kansas City sporting house. Now, seeing one of the patrol wave his arm at the head of the train, Porter drew his pistol and shot to death the two rearguard riders who, tumbling from their horses, were still smiling at his story.

Meanwhile, Purvis Jellicoe had shot Tyrone McCone off his horse, and his fellow "soldiers" had gunned down Delehanty and Soames. The surprise was total as the Jellicoes blistered the wagon train with their fast repeating Spencers.

Tyrone McCone, with an expression of final chagrin on his face, had hurtled from his horse, landing painfully, but still effective. He rose, slipping in a fresh, steaming pile of horse manure just dropped by his own mount, and opened fire. To no avail. A wave of bullets cut him to the trail.

It was over in a few minutes. The riders swept in, their screams and the frenzy of their attack all but paralyzing the defenders of the wagon train, save the hardiest veterans and the freshly dead. Shortly the last survivor had been accounted for.

There was a big grin on Porter Jellicoe's face when it was all over and he rode back to where the "soldiers" were collected.

Purvis Jellicoe unbuttoned his army tunic. He was not smiling. He suddenly swung to the others. "You boys, you get your lazy asses movin'. Prior, you take up this end, then Poon an' Porter ride flank, and Print an' Palmer, you be down t' other end. Space yourselves. Check everythin'. An' remember, there'll be strick accountin' back to home!" He sniffed, then jabbed his little finger up his right nostril to remove some obstruction.

The five kneed their horses and hurried to their work.

Porter Jellicoe grinned as he said, "She went like a greased goose, Paw."

The old man leaned on his saddlehorn. "*I* will tell *you* how it went, mister, and don't you never forget that. Now get your ass moving and clean out them wagons. I mean I want it done fast!"

The work went quickly under the burning vigilance of Old Man Jellicoe. When it was finished, he called his five sons to him.

"Now, you get the evidence around. Make sure there wasn't no slip-up with some stupid fool riding a horse with shoes. And I want them arrers put about. You get the right ones, Prior, the Cheyenne—them with the butt ends whittled to a sharp edge, and with the right colors. And the whiskey too."

The buzzards had already started to coast in when the party finished and rode back across the creek, leaving the dead bodies, scalped and mutilated, and the wagons smoldering in the high, clean air.

eleven _____

Matt Kincaid rode to the lip of the long draw and drew rein. With exquisite care his eyes swept the countryside. Beside him, sitting the little blue roan gelding, Windy Mandalian chewed pensively on his eternal plug of tobacco. The great plain lay before them like an enormous brown carpet, the grass dry and brittle from lack of rain.

"Dry enough you can hear it," Windy said.

Both the men had now fixed their searching eyes on a strip of trees lining a winding creek at some distance to their north.

"There they be," Windy said.

Kincaid took out his glasses and focused on the distant figures circling in the air beyond the creek.

"Vultures," he muttered.

"That's the size of it." Windy rubbed the end of his nose with the palm of his hand. "Nose itches. Sign of something, ain't it?"

"Maybe you're going to get laid." Matt spoke without taking his eyes away from the field glasses.

"That's the best news I heard in a whole month," Windy said. "Here comes Drags-His-Foot."

The Delaware scout, who had ridden ahead of the patrol to reconnoiter, was pounding out of the trees by the creek, whipping his pony with his riding quirt while he lay flat along its stretched back.

"He has found it for sure," Windy said. "Him and them buzzards." He was referring to the massacred wagon train, news of which had reached Outpost Number Nine through Tipi Town, the friendlies' neighboring camp, which was Windy's principal source of information and gossip on the plains.

The scout took the glasses that Kincaid handed him now, and raised them to his eyes. Grunting, he shifted his weight with the roan as it whiffled and, stretching out its right foreleg, rubbed its muzzle and then its long blazed nose against it. Then it raised its head and shook it, its mane flying.

"Can't see much more'n I can see with the naked eye," Windy said, his tone sour.

Behind them waited First Platoon of Easy Company, the men muttering, reaching for their canteens, the horses shaking their heads, swishing their tails, biting at the ticks that were feeding on the creases in their bodies.

The Delaware was laid out on his pony like a piece of rawhide string, the hooves drumming louder on the dry, hard ground as man and horse raced toward the waiting patrol. Pulling up hard in a cloud of dust, without any expression on his face, Drags-His-Foot said one word.

"Rubout."

"Cheyenne?"

Drags-His-Foot handed Windy the arrow he had brought. Windy studied it for a moment, then said to

96

Kincaid, "See how that butt end is whittled to a sharp ridge, the string notch right center in the ridge? And see the butt tapering to the shaft, and the triangle head with exact straight sides." He paused to spit, raising his head to look at Gatwin and two or three other soldiers who had drawn closer to hear what he was saying about the arrow.

"You young fellows better know whose arrow is whose," he went on. "Like this here being Cheyenne." He looked at Matt Kincaid, who nodded, shifting his weight.

"Like Crow arrows is different," Windy continued. "They're some like this here, excepting they're always thick in the shaft. This here is slender. Then you see, too, the Cheyenne don't use barbs on their arrows, like the Sioux."

"Sir, can I ask a question?" Gatwin's horse took a small step toward the scout, but its rider had his eyes on Kincaid.

"Shoot."

"What are those wavy lines running from the head to the feathers? Does that mean something, or is it just to make it special in some way?"

Matt looked at Windy. "Well, scout?"

"Those wavy lines, there're three of 'em, right? See how even they are? They ain't just decoration. With the Indian, everything has some kind of meaning. May be crazy to us civilized folks, but they take it all serious. Like these lines is for communicating with the Great Spirit. They claim the good medicine flows along wavy lines."

When Gatwin moved his hand slightly, Windy handed him the arrow. Kincaid watched him studying it. Nodding, Gatwin handed it back to the scout. "Thank you, Mr. Mandalian," he said.

Windy slapped a grin onto his face. "Just call me Professor," he said. He turned to Drags-His-Foot. "Notice anything special?"

"All dead. Scalped. Wagons burned."

"Figures."

Kincaid kicked his horse into a turn. 'Sergeant Olsen!"

"Sir!" Gus Olsen kneed his mount forward.

"We will ride in with the first and second squads, right and left, guiding on those two tallest trees. The third squad will hold center on this side of the creek until we've crossed and seen the situation. You will be in charge of the third squad, Sergeant."

"Yessir!"

The salutes were swift, and at a bark from Olsen, saddles creaked, bits jangled, horses broke wind, and a couple of mounts spooked as the patrol got ready to move out.

Kincaid turned to Drags-His-Foot. "You ride with the sergeant."

Without a word the Delaware turned his pony and trotted toward Olsen and his men.

At the rear of the first squad, Malone threw an appraising eye at young Gatwin. "Well, son, this is it. Hope you got a strong stomach."

Private Gatwin said nothing, only bit his lower lip. He raised himself slightly in his stirrups now to shift his weight in the painful McClellan saddle, wishing that Malone would not take the annoying attitude that he was such a greenhorn.

Still, it was good to be in First Platoon along with Lieutenant Kincaid and Windy Mandalian. He was lucky, all right. Now, as the command broke from the lieutenant to ride, Gatwin kicked his bay horse, feeling the sudden surge of power between his legs as the three squads comprising First Platoon trotted out across the plain toward the line of cottonwood trees and Jack Creek.

Kincaid had given orders to ride in at the trot; he didn't want the horses tired when he got there, so he kept the pace down. In just a short while the platoon had reached the trees. The first and second squads rode through to the creek, while Gus Olsen and the third held their position in the protection of the cottonwoods, to cover the rest of the platoon.

The lead horses splashed across the shallow creek, the water breaking fast around their hocks as they picked their way across. Gatwin's mount spooked and he almost lost his seat, but the moment was a good one. He had been dreaming about what he would find ahead, and his unexpected loss of balance brought him right into the present.

At a signal from Kincaid, they walked their horses toward the grisly tableau that lay before them. Gatwin was vaguely aware of the second squad riding in from the left; then the stench hit him and he was aware of nothing but the scene that met his eyes.

It didn't seem as if it could be real—the blood, the split and torn bodies, the smoldering wagons, the relentless stench soaking into him. There were some dead horses, one lying with its foreleg raised grotesquely in the air. A man's head had been cut from his body and it lay beside him like a parcel waiting for him to awaken and pick it up.

A woman lay naked with a bloody smear between her legs, while in her arms she clutched a small bundle.

"Looks like they scalped her crotch," Malone said at Gatwin's elbows.

Gatwin turned his head just in time to vomit everything he had in him.

"Better get shut of it all at once," Malone said soberly, his own face none too ruddy as he spoke.

Al Gatwin's eyes were stinging, his legs had gone cold. The bundle in the woman's arms, he now saw, was a baby. His head swam and he felt that something inside it was going to fly off.

"All right," he heard the lieutenant saying. "Take a moment. Remember it. And then put it away and we'll get to work."

Gatwin realized he had been staring at a man who had been castrated and his genitals shoved into his mouth. An arrow protruded from each of his eye sockets.

Suddenly his head cleared and he found he was able to look at it. He turned toward Malone, glad the big Irishman was there, thankful for his words now, and no longer irritated.

"God almighty, Malone..."

Malone said softly, "Don't forget it, young feller. That could easily be you or me."

The order had been given to dismount and hold the horses while a burial detail got ready. Kincaid, Mandalian, and Drags-His-Foot, who had been signaled in from the third squad, were examining the bodies, the ground, the burned wagons, as they reconstructed what had taken place. Meanwhile, Olsen's men had moved out of the trees and were now guarding the perimeter around the site of the massacre.

"We'll be digging pretty directly now," Malone said. "It'll be good to get to work. Better than standing about scratching our asses."

Stretch Dobbs, all six feet seven inches of him, approached, his Adam's apple pumping up and down fast in his long, skinny throat. "Jesus," he said. "Jesus Christ!"

"You've seen it before, Dobbsy."

"Malone, I never want to see it again."

"I'll second that."

Dobbs lowered his voice toward the Irishman. 'How's the kid taking it?"

"Same as all of us."

All Gatwin knew he didn't want to know what it was he was looking at, yet he couldn't take his eyes away. Now he realized it was a hand, a hand without any body attached to it. It was, he saw, a man's left hand, and it was holding a piece of paper. Or was it a picture? Someone's picture? At that point his stomach began to heave again, but nothing came up.

A few feet away, Kincaid said to Windy Mandalian's back, "Those arrows were shot into them after they were killed."

The scout had squatted and was looking at a stone tomahawk lying next to a coup stick. "And this coup stick and tomahawk was put here after the fighting," he said.

"How so?"

"No dead Indian with it."

"But they take their dead with them."

"Yup. But why leave the coup stick?"

"You think it was the Contraries again?"

"Or maybe whites dressed up as Indians."

"That's getting to be pretty popular," Matt said. "I didn't see any tracks of shod horses."

"They've gotten smart enough for that," Windy said. "But that coup stick—I dunno." He stood up. "Maybe whites, maybe Cheyenne. A small party—six, I'd say."

"Looks like they got in real close," Matt said.

Windy grinned. "How'd you figure that?"

"The emigrants must have been caught off guard. There were a lot more of them than whoever it was hit the train."

"So they should've been able to stand 'em off," Windy said, picking it up. "Why didn't they? How were they tricked so easy?"

The scout walked over to one of the scalped bodies, and squatted. "Done a fair to decent job of lifting his hair. Could've been kids, you know, out on a revenge raid or something."

"Because of Deal and his shooting that Cheyenne, you mean?"

"I don't mean nothing. I'm just studying it." Windy suddenly turned his head slightly and blew his nose, pressing his thumb first against one nostril, then the other.

He looked down at his thumbnail, then reached up and scratched with his little finger deep into his ear.

"That vicious?" He seemed to be asking the question to the ground. "I dunno. Faraway Eagle has to be the closest to it—and to the Contraries." He paused; Matt thought he was gathering spittle, for his mouth was working, but it was words. "This was no ordinary rubout," Windy said.

"Unless another band of Cheyenne have come into the territory," Matt suggested.

"Maybe. Maybe another band unbeknownst even to Faraway Eagle. Shit, Matt, we both know the Cheyenne from way back. They ain't no Sweet Jesuses, that's a cinch; but they don't do like Preacher Chivington, neither."

"Unless they were whiskeyed up?" Matt nodded toward a jug lying near the body of one of the emigrants, and walked over and picked it up and sniffed at it.

"Maybe. Maybe," Windy said. "But we know too that Faraway Eagle has always been opposed to whiskey-drinking."

"Maybe some kids, some young warriors got hold of it," Matt said.

"That's the idea."

The two of them had been moving slowly through the scene of the massacre, speaking most of the time without looking directly at each other, musing aloud, trying to piece it together.

Suddenly Matt saw the scout squat down beside the

body of a woman. Her skirt had been pulled up over her head, and she had been raped and mutilated. Windy was trying to pry open the woman's hand.

"Shit, she's clamped on to it like a bear trap," he said as Kincaid approached.

Together they finally managed to open the dead woman's hand. But it was empty.

"Dunno," Windy said. "Just had a notion she might've grabbed something while he was raping her."

He rose and turned away, and now the two of them watched the men of the patrol collecting the bodies. They were standing there in silence when two enlisted men approached to pick up the body of the woman for burial.

"Hold 'er just a minute," Windy said. He was picking something out of one of his side teeth with his thumbnail.

Kincaid looked at the tall scout. He knew Windy was a man who played hunches, and he studied him now as he squinted up at the sky, his eyes on the circling buzzards, then looked down at the toe of his boot, while the two enlisted men waited.

"It's how they got in that close that stumps me, Matt." And all at once he turned back to the body of the woman and dropped down beside it. Matt saw that he was studying the woman's face; her mouth was drawn back in a grimace.

Suddenly Windy reached over and tried to force her jaws apart. "Gimme something to pry with," he said. "I can't move it." Before Matt could say anything, Windy had pulled out his own skinning knife and, with a few deft strokes, pried the woman's jaws apart. Reaching inside, he withdrew something that Matt couldn't see.

"What have you got?"

"This." Windy stood up and opened his hand. Lying on his palm was a button from a United States Army uniform.

twelve

"Stupid! Just plumb stupid and lookin' for it, by God!"

Old Man Jellicoe was furious as he clomped bare-footed about the dirt floor of the cabin, bottle in hand, his forefinger pointing like a piece of goat horn at his recalcitrant son Poon.

"You want to get us all stretched, you fuckin' ass-hole?" He waved his arms, spilling whiskey, and his shadow, thrown upon the sod walls by the light of two coal-oil lamps, made a grotesque shadow.

His whiskey-bright eyes slid over his other four sons, who, with Poon, were slouching about the cabin. They had just finished supper and were about to start up some poker, and maybe a little more drinking.

"Don't you damn fools know that sonofabitch Man-dalian will pick up that coup stick quicker'n any of you can scratch your left ball!" He drank furiously, some of the brown fluid slopping onto his filthy yellow-white beard, but he ignored it.

"Paw, how come you know that Mandalian feller, or whatever his name is?" asked Porter, hoping to change the subject.

"Don't know him personal. But I know his kind. From the old days."

"Was he one of them with Quantrill and Anderson?" Prior asked.

"Who?"

"Mandalian."

"Told you I never knew the feller, you asshole. Said I know his kind. No—no, he ain't like Quantrill or Bloody Bill. He is a smart one. Heerd of him when I was over on the Hoodoo range. Don't matter, what I am trying to get through your thick heads is he is one smart sonofabitch and that is why we cannot leave any mistakes lying about."

"Exceptin' for that coup stick, I think we covered pretty good, Paw," said Palmer Jellicoe, the next youngest to Poon.

"You think they might suspicion it wasn't Indians?" Prior asked.

"Mebbe," said his brother Print. "But mebbe we'll be lucky." He sniffed. "Leastways, they can't put anything on us. We got everything well stashed."

"Thing is, we'll lie low a bit now," the old man said. "Maybe get a little whiskey to the Injuns so's the suspicion will be on them. Time we pull our next raid, the army and everyone'll figger it's drunk savages doin' the damage." He chuckled. His grin widened, and he showed his large, spaced teeth as the mirth caught him, shaking him, squeezing him to a great wheeling of laughter, the tears pouring down his carved old face. "Boys," he gasped, "we're gonna be rich. I told you. This here is the gold mine. Not out in California or up in Alder Gulch or

106

Virginia City or any of them places. But right here on the way to Oregon, with them emigrants coming along like a bunch of locusts. We got the best pickings we could ever. And your old man done it. *Is* doin' it, by God! By God, Purvis Jellicoe, ain't he a one! And listen, we'll build our own spread here. Jellicoe City, just like I said. Them fuckin' Yankees can't stop us. They won't. We'll kill 'em all!" He stood swaying in the middle of the room, panting, staring wildly at his five sons.

"Paw, that sounds real good!"

"Like it used to be, Paw, that how you mean?"

"Used to be?"

"When you rode with Quantrill, Paw, and killed all them Jayhawkers."

There was a big grin on their sire's face. Ah, it was good when the boys honored the past like this. They'd been too young, but he, Purvis—why, hell, he'd been through it all. His head was again swimming with the pictures, the words, the gunshots, the shouting, the twisting agonies and the sweet pleasures, and the riding and whoring and drinking. Where was it all now? By God, it was right here. He, Purvis Jellicoe, was bringing it for his boys, so that they too would know the glory days.

Laughter crashed suddenly out of his wrinkled throat. He was no longer standing in the middle of the cabin. "There we was! You young assholes got no idea the way it was. There we was, the day Quantrill rode into Lawrence, Kansas, on his spanky little claybank gelding, and by God if he didn't order every male shot to death and their houses burned, and I mean right now!" He paused, his russet eyes sweeping them. "Know how many?"

"One hundred eighty," said Palmer gleefully.

"One hundred eighty-*two!*" roared the old man. "And we done it. Us and Quantrill! I was right there with him!"

"Tell about Bloody Bill, Paw," Print said. "He wasn't no lollygaggin' sissy, was he!"

107

"He wasn't no Quantrill, not by a long shot. But Bill was something. He was something, he was." The old man took a drink from the bottle and tossed it to Poon. "Drink, you puppy. You're too soft, you got cotton in your balls! Drink, goddamn you!" And suddenly he was furious, standing as rigid as a corral post in front of his youngest, the one he always accused of being "soft, soft like your Ma."

Smiling, Poon, with his elbow on the table, drew the bottle to his lips and drank. But suddenly he gagged and the whiskey poured out of his mouth, and he was coughing, bent over double, his face crimson with the effort.

"Asshole!" roared his father. "You wouldn't last ten minutes with Bill Anderson. None of you would! Shit! I mind the time we hit that railroad train at Centralia. Found twenty-six Union troops on board. Know what we did?"

They nodded. They had all heard it many, many times, but somehow none of them ever tired of the stories.

"We by God lined them twenty-six soldier boys up alongside the railroad track and shot 'em. Shot 'em dead, dead, dead!"

He stood with great effort now, for he had drunk a lot, even for him. Pausing now, he scratched vigorously at each buttock, then in his baggy crotch, his dirt-lined face wreathed in pleasure.

"Scratch it more'n three times, you're playin' with it, Paw," Prior Jellicoe said, and all laughed at that, including their sire.

But Poon, recovered from his coughing attack, couldn't leave well enough alone. He had never learned the foolishness of trying to explain things to his father.

"But Paw," he said, "you told us to leave Cheyenne stuff about. That coup stick was from a real Cheyenne, that one we shot over on the Green River when we took his hoss that time."

The old man spat hugely on the dirt floor, and then he spat again, hitting the first glob dead center. "Well, looky here," he said in unfeigned self-admiration at his accuracy. But his mood swept back to his irritation at Poon and his mistake.

"Danged fools, the lot of you—I can't even allow you to think. How did I ever get such assholes for sons? I can't explain it. If the Almighty up in His heaven was to ask me that question, I'd just have to say I dunno. Don't you buggers know that them Injuns never leave their special stuff just lying around? After they do all their killing and raping, they take away their dead ones— and all them weapons and sticks and stuff, so they get buried with the dead one. Only time you find one of them sticks is with its owner right alongside it."

"And that scout feller will find it," said Prior, and looked over at his brother Poon.

"Next time we'll play it tighter, Poon," Print said.

"Go fuck yourself," Poon said.

Print had been sitting on a crate, and now it went flying as he stood, kicking it out of the way. "You little shit, I'll whip your ass from here to breakfast!"

Suddenly a pistol shot cracked into the room, and all froze.

"That'll be enough," Paw said returning his smoking hogleg to its holster. "You young fellers run afoul of Purvis Jellicoe, I'd feel real sorry for you. So behave. You boys behave, on account of I need you for my next plan."

At his words, their faces lit up.

"You got a new one planned, Paw?"

"Maybe."

"Paw, this time there won't be no slip-ups."

"That I know," their father said, and he patted the big sixgun at his right hip.

They had all seated themselves again, and now, a

good deal sobered, Purvis stood before them.

"Paw, you gonna tell us the plan?"

"Might." He sniffed. He scratched his crotch again, his fingers delving. "Maybe time for a bath," he said with a grin. "Ain't had one since we treed Honeytown."

"That was a town with fine hospitality," Palmer said.

"What we'll have here, boys! We get our stake, some whiskey to the right places, and a few more raids, and we'll have her. Then it'll be Jellicoe City. Like down in Missouri."

"But what about the army, Paw?"

"Easy enough to get them papers and make the soldiers happy. No sweat there." He paused, a thought seeming to occur to him, for his brow wrinkled.

Suddenly he let out a roar. "But, you assholes, none of you never did see the real dumb mistake you made! You don't even notice it! Not even now we been jawing this good while!"

"What's that, Paw? Thought everything was all right except for that stick?"

"You fools! The really dumb thing you done wasn't leaving that stick there, but not bringing home some women. What the hell you assholes figure we are gonna do for pussy around this place? I ain't got a mind to be putting calluses on my fucking hand!"

Seated backwards on their horses, they rode in a circle around the camp. This was in the late evening, and the last of the sun's rays were reaching up from beyond the western horizon, shooting into the velvet sky. Nearby, the grazing bells of the pony herd sounded, and chickadees and blue jays flew quickly to their rendezvous, while the smoke from the cookfires rose, disappearing toward the evening star.

They had run their horses as they sat them backwards, and now they walked them. Some of the riders wore women's robes, some were naked and covered with mud, some wore masks. All were costumed in outrageous ways.

"We will tell you a story about someone we will call Prairie Dog," began one of the riders.

"One time," another rider said, "Prairie Dog showed how he could lie."

And a third continued the story, "Prairie Dog came into a camp where there were some tipis. The men were all sitting around. They knew Prairie Dog was always telling lies."

Another rider picked up the story, and now, as they rode, they took turns telling a part of the story about Prairie Dog.

"The men called Prairie Dog over."

"'Prairie Dog,' they said, 'you are the biggest liar we've ever known.'"

"'How do you know I lie?'"

"'Oh, you always make trouble when you lie. You get away with things like that. You are very good at it. Why don't you teach us how to lie so we can lie successfully too.'"

"'Well,'" said Prairie Dog, "'I had to pay a big price for that power. I learned it from my enemy.'"

"'What did you pay?'"

"'One horse. But it was my best buffalo horse, and it had a fine bridle.'"

"'Is that all?'"

"'Yes.'"

"They did not think that was much, for in those days there were plenty of horses. One man brought out a fine white buffalo horse, his best."

"'Yes,' said Prairie Dog. 'This is a good-looking horse. This is the kind I mean. It was with a horse like this that I paid for my power.'"

"Then Prairie Dog said, 'Let me try the horse. If he doesn't buck, I'll explain my power.'"

111

"They agreed, and Prairie Dog got up on the horse. Prairie Dog had never been on a horse before, and he dug in his claws to hold on. The horse began to buck."

"'Oh, this horse needs a blanket, that's the trouble,' said Prairie Dog."

"They put a blanket on the horse."

"But Prairie Dog's claws were sharp and they went through the blanket and the horse jumped again."

"'Oh, he wants something more over his back. He wants a good saddle on.'"

"So they got a good saddle and helped Prairie Dog put it on the horse. Prairie Dog got on again and then turned his head as though he were listening to something."

"'That is my power speaking,' he said. 'That voice tells me he wants a whip too.'"

"They gave him one."

"He said, 'I'm going around now and try this horse to see if he still bucks. I'll come right back and tell you about it.'"

"He rode off a little way and then turned around and shouted back, 'This is the way I lie. I get people to give me horses and blankets and saddles and other fine things.'"

"Then he rode away."

"The people couldn't do anything about it. Prairie Dog went home and showed his wife what he had."

"'Look at this fine horse,' he said. 'I took it away from an enemy out of the plains. It was some fight.'"

"But Prairie Dog did not know how to take care of the horse. When he got off, the horse walked away and went back to its owner."

By the time the story about Prairie Dog was finished, there were more stars in the sky, and now the mothers called their children into the lodges and told them it was time to sleep.

Outside in the starlit night the Contraries danced, telling each other what a beautiful day it was, how hot the sun felt on their faces and hands, often speaking the words backwards too, and none of them forgetting that this was what they each had sworn to do.

Faraway Eagle walked slowly through the camp. As he passed silently, heads turned to see him. He had watched the people listening to the story about the trickster Prairie Dog.

It was well, he was thinking, that the people could still listen to stories, that the Contrary Ones could still follow their ways, although he knew the missionaries and other whites had often complained and had even tried to forbid much of the Contrary dancing.

Entering his lodge, he saw that the fire had been lighted. He seated himself and began preparing his pipe. When the pipe was ready, he offered it to the four directions, and then, taking a small buffalo chip from the fire, he lighted it.

Tomorrow, he decided, he would go to the high place that he had known for a very long time, and he would cry for help. It was a good time for that. He had not visited the high place where he had last dreamed for a long time.

He had closed his eyes, not to sleep, but to see better into the place where real things happened, when he felt the drumming of horses in the ground beneath him. He opened his eyes as one of the Dog Soldiers came to tell of the arrival of scouts with strong news.

The two scouts had sweat all over their bodies. Listening in the soft firelight, with the tribal headmen seated in a circle, Faraway Eagle closed his eyes. He was trying to see, trying to feel in his mind and body the way it had happened.

"It was at Jack Creek," the scouts said. "All the wagons were burned, the horses run off, taken, or killed, and the men and women and children all dead."

113

"Was it the men with the whiskey?" one of the headmen asked.

"No," said Blue Foot, one of the scouts, "it was whites dressed up as soldiers so they could come close to the men in the wagons, who were more numerous than they. Then they fired arrows and left things lying around to make it look like it was the People who had done this thing."

"Cheyenne arrows?"

"Yes, they left the arrows." Dog Falls Over, the second scout, handed the chief one of the arrows taken from the emigrant train.

"The soldier lieutenant knows of this?" Faraway Eagle asked.

"He came with Windy and the soldiers. Many soldiers. They came quickly and we had to hide. We watched them."

"And did they see it was not the People who had done this thing?"

"They saw it," said Blue Foot. "There was a coup stick which the raiders left there, and we did not take it so that the *veho* would know this."

"It is well," Faraway Eagle said. "It is always better to show than to tell, for in telling there is always doubt."

"Who could the soldiers be who did the fighting?" asked one of the headmen.

"Clearly, it must be the Gray Men dressed as soldiers to fool the others, to surprise them," said Faraway Eagle. "Those men who have moved in near Gooseberry Creek." He looked at the two scouts. "Was there whiskey?"

"There was some," said Dog Falls Over.

"But the People will be blamed," someone said from the circle of headmen.

But Faraway Eagle, catching something in the speaker's voice, held up his hand. "When we are blamed, then we will be blamed," he said.

thirteen ─────────────

"So we're pretty damn sure it's the Jellicoes, but we can't prove anything." Conway was standing in the middle of the parade with Kincaid and Windy Mandalian.

The patrol had just returned from Jack Creek and a visit to the Jellicoes, and the men, hot and weary, had been dismissed.

"That's the way it adds up to me, sir," Matt said. "The Jellicoes were clean and innocent as a baby's eyes."

Conway half turned to Windy. "You feel the same, do you?"

"That is who it looks to be, Captain." The scout hooked one thumb in his belt, looking at the officer from beneath the brim of his hat. "Them Jellicoes is bad apples. Like I said, the old man used to ride with Quantrill and Bloody Bill Anderson."

"And his boys are chips off the old block, is that it?"

"That's it, Captain. I'd swear on a stack of Indian maidens the Cheyenne had nothing to do with that rubout.

Only other possibility would be someone from outside the territory coming in."

"What about whiskey? Was there any sign of whiskey about?"

"We picked up a couple of empty jugs," Matt said. "But they could have been planted."

"To make it look like drunken Indians?"

"Right, sir."

They had reached the far side of the parade, and now Conway said, "Let's have some coffee, then I'll let you get some rest."

When they walked into the mess hall they found a dejected Dutch Rothausen. His cheeks were pale, he moved in a dreamy way, his eyes were streaked with red lines.

"Coffee, Sergeant. We'd like three cups of your best."

"Yes, sir."

In a moment Rothausen was back with three mugs of steaming coffee, which he set on the long table where the men had seated themselves.

Conway sighed as he raised his mug. "Coffee wipes away a lot of trouble, wouldn't you say?" He drank, and his face suddenly changed its expression.

Matt, noting his reaction, raised his own cup and sipped. Controlling the expletive that rose to his tongue, he put the cup down and said, 'Something's happened."

"Tastes like owl piss," was Windy's succinct comment.

"Sergeant, what have you got in this concoction?" demanded Conway. "It tastes like soap!"

Rothausen, wincing under the captain's words, approached dolefully. "Sir, it's the new recipe."

"New recipe? Why did you change to a new recipe? We'd all gotten used to the old one. It was at least possible to drink!" Conway pushed his mug away from him.

"Sir, the new recipe is from Mrs. Dodgson."

"Mrs. Dodgson!"

"Sir, she said the coffee tasted, well, 'foul' was the word she used. And she said we had to try this new way of making it."

Conway's lips were a thin line as he looked at Kincaid and Windy Mandalian. "Christ," he muttered softly. "God Almighty!" Then, returning to the full power of his rank, he said, "Take this swill away, Sergeant Rothausen, and make us an *old* batch of coffee! The *old,* the *former, foul* kind of coffee!"

"Yessir. Coming right up, sir." And Dutch was unable to hold back the start of a smile on his big face as he quickly collected the mugs.

By the time the mess sergeant returned with fresh coffee, the three were deep in conversation.

"Remember," Conway was saying, "that Deal and the girl Nellie thought the Cheyenne were drunk when they had that business over the mule. I mean, how do you know it wasn't drunk Cheyenne dressed up as soldiers? Why whites?"

"You're suggesting the Indians could have left the coup stick on purpose to make it look like a mistake, and so implicate whites, sir?"

Conway nodded. "I mean, those Contraries, as I understand them—and I have to admit I don't understand much—they do everything backwards and upside down." He nodded toward Windy. "You say the Cheyenne aren't that destructive, or at least had no reason to be in this instance, but how do we know it wasn't the Contraries? For instance, they could have shot arrows into dead men and women, pretending they were still alive."

Windy looked at Kincaid with a big grin on his face. "Shit, Matt, now I know why you got him for a CO. He don't let nothing get by."

"Damn good thing he doesn't," Matt said.

Windy took the used plug of tobacco out of his mouth and tossed it out the open door onto the parade.

Conway's eyebrows shot up. "Something wrong, scout?"

"Just clearin' my pipes so I can talk it out better," Windy said with a wink at Kincaid.

"Let's have it," Conway sighed, lifting his new cup of coffee. "Ah, that's more like it."

His companions, sampling the fresh brew, agreed.

"See, the thing is, Captain, if it was the Contraries, then the only possible reason for the attack would've been on account of that feller getting shot in the leg at Owl Creek."

"And it's too much," Conway added.

"It is too much. They would never go that far."

"I'm inclined to agree. Mind you, Windy, I'm going through it because we've got to be sure of our ground."

"Gotcha. See, the trouble with the Contraries is they're a secret society." He lifted his hands off the table, shrugging. "That means *everything's* secret, right?"

"Right."

"I mean, not even the tribes know much about them. They don't look at things the way normal people do, and they for sure don't act normal."

"Well, what the hell are they, then?" Conway leaned back, throwing a glance at Matt, who looked equally puzzled. "All I know is what I've heard, mostly from you, that they do things backwards—eat with their other hand, walk backwards, and all that sort of thing."

"That is so," Windy said, "but not always. The tribes have different kinds of Contraries. For instance, the Sioux have the *heyoka* clown. He's a clown, and he's got vision, greater vision than anybody. Broken Leg, an old friend of mine, told me these clowns are religious— they're considered holy by the tribe. Fooling around the way they do is a way of seeing the world differently,

118

was how Broken Leg put it. So they shake everything up. He said he was visiting the Cheyenne once and the Contraries were there. They asked him if he was hungry, and he said yes. Then they asked what he'd like to eat, and he said food, so they brought him a bowl of dogshit."

Windy chuckled. "Broken Leg caught on fast. He said no, he'd made a mistake, he didn't want food, he wanted shit. So they brought him food."

"It's clear you've got to be careful what you say around those fellows."

"They're trying to shake everybody up, is that it?" said Matt.

"The way I understand it, they're showing a different way of looking at things—kind of a way to make a man really sharp. You know how the Sioux, and the Cheyenne too, are always telling their warriors to 'be attentive.' I've heard that a whole hell of a lot of times around them fellers." He paused, then went on, "You got to know all your habits, everything you do and think, even how you speak—if you're going to do it all backwards." Windy cleared his throat, feeling the end of his nose with his fingers. "You know what I figure it is? It's like those games kids play when they turn one of the bunch around until he's dizzy and he don't know where he is. Then they change everything in the place, so that when he gets his bearings he don't know where he is at all; he's plumb lost and then he has to find out where he is, and maybe even *who* he is. Like that." Windy pulled out his cut-plug and skinning knife. "Shit, all I can say is, it must be one hell of a job, remembering to do everything ass-end-frontwards."

"But they do that all day long?" asked Conway. "They must make a lot of mistakes."

"Dunno," Windy said. "See, again, it's secret. Probably they do it mostly for ceremonies, at special times. When they have to fight—and I don't believe they do fight much, 'less they have to—then they fight regular. But I'm not sure." He paused, grinning. "Fact is, that's about the only thing the Indians do that I can't understand at all."

"What about this proposed knife fight between Ethan Deal and one of the Contraries, Matt? How do you see that?" Conway asked.

"Sir, I don't see Deal having a prayer in that encounter, no matter how old his opponent is."

"So what can we do?"

"I have an idea, sir, but I'd like your permission to hold on to it a day or two till I get it set. I still haven't figured Deal out, and I feel the need to do so."

There was a smile in Conway's eyes as he looked at his adjutant and nodded. "Permission granted, Lieutenant." He tossed off the rest of his coffee. "Deal—yes, he does take a bit of figuring. I, for one, don't believe that confession of his."

"I think he doesn't know what happened, sir."

"Windy?" Conway turned to the scout, raising his eyebrows in question.

"I don't believe he done it, Captain. Think he must've got out of his head when he come to. Like you've said yourself. On the other hand..."

Conway leaned forward on the table, his eyes straight on the scout. "On the other hand—what?"

"I dunno."

Conway held his eyes on Windy for a moment, then swung them to Matt Kincaid. "I'd say we all three do know, only it hasn't quite started to bubble yet. I'd say we all three have a feeling in our bones that the man is still lying."

"This here is cottonwood," Windy was saying. They were again sitting on the steps of the sutler's store, but this time both were whittling, the boy with a knife the scout had given him, and Windy with his barlow.

"You know, for the tribes, each tree up here on the High Plains had got its special use." Windy spat at nothing at all, not even raising his eyes from his whittling. "They make arrows with the chokecherry. They cut dogwood into tipi stakes, and ash they make pipestems out of." He looked over at the boy. "You catching what I'm saying?"

To his surprise the boy didn't nod, but raised his hand in the sign for "yes."

"Well, good enough. Glad our lessons is bearing fruit. You'll be able to talk to the Indians and me, if nobody else, leastways."

The boy had returned to his whittling, and Windy watched him for a moment longer.

"You take this cottonwood now—it grows along the river bottoms. The tribes build lodges out of cottonwood—that is, the Mandan and the Pawnee once done so. And there is even food for the ponies in the cottonwood when there's a hard winter. And you know what? They make a kind of candy cream from the inside bark. Tastes real good. Maybe we'll get you some one day."

Pop Evans, the sutler, stood in the doorway. "A slow day," he grumbled.

"You ain't gonna dwindle away and starve, Pop," Windy said, his eyes on the sutler's big belly.

"Nor yourself," Pop replied sourly.

"You got any cut-plug in there?"

"All you got money to pay for."

"Shit," said Windy. "Thought you was gonna say, 'Hell, yes, Windy old boy, we got all the cut-plug you want.'"

Even Pop Evans had to chuckle at that, his jowls jiggling, his cheeks reddening. He sighed, and his body seemed to exert a great effort as he shifted his weight.

Windy stood up and followed him into the store, saying over his shoulder to the boy, "See if this man's got any decent chewin' stuff."

The boy got quickly to his feet and followed.

It was gloomy in the store, as it always was, though it was possible to find things. A half-dozen enlisted men lounged in the chairs. Some were drinking beer, others were smoking, and one or two were just doing nothing. The place smelled of oil, leather, tobacco, three-point-two beer, and sweet stuff.

Windy bought his cut-plug. As he paid the sutler he noticed the boy standing in front of a large apothecary jar, so close the bill of his cap was touching the glass.

"Got rock candy in there, have you?" the scout asked.

"Yes, Windy, my friend, all you want."

They both chuckled at that.

"I do believe the young man there would like some," Pop said.

"How'd you ever figure that?" Windy said, reaching again into his pocket.

The boy looked up then, his eyes large and clear, and there was the suspicion of a grin on his face.

Windy moved his hands in sign language. "You want some?"

And the boy replied, his fingers and hands moving not as quickly as the man's, but fast enough to bring a grin to Windy's face.

"You learn fast," Windy said.

"It's on me," Pop Evans said, opening the jar.

A stunned silence fell in the room.

Malone, Dobbs, Gatwin, Harvey Barker, and the two other enlisted men in the store turned, their mouths open in huge surprise.

"Looks like you stopped the merry-go-round, Pop," Windy said, grinning broadly.

"Goddammit, can't a man give a kid a piece of candy without you damn fools acting like he'd stole somebody's daughter?"

A roar of laughter rose at that.

As Windy walked away, he winked at the sutler. "Always knew you had a good heart, Pop."

"So did I," said Pop.

"Only one thing burns my ass."

"What's that, Windy?"

Windy held his palm toward the floor, just below his right buttock. "A fire about this high."

Again they sat on the steps, but now Gatwin and Barker had joined them.

"You boys whittle?" Windy asked.

"No, I never," said Barker.

"I used to, some, when I was a kid." Al Gatwin was looking at the boy. "You look like you're doing it right," he said.

Zachary said nothing.

"You got to talk to him in sign language," Windy said. "I been teaching him. You want to learn?"

"You mean, what the Indians use?"

"Yup." He put down his knife and the piece of cottonwood, and with his right index finger and thumb he formed an incomplete circle, with the back of his hand up; then he extended his arm horizontally, pointing across his body to the left, and raised his hand about a foot. "That means sunrise," he said.

The two enlisted men tried it, while Windy corrected them.

"Zack, you show 'em the sign for heart."

The boy hesitated a moment, then put down his whittling and, compressing his right hand so that all his fingers were tight together, with the thumb behind them, he pointed it downward over his heart, the palm in.

"Good," Windy said with a grin. He showed them

some more signs, and finally he asked Zachary to show the sign for possession. The boy held his closed fist up in front of his neck, its back to the right, then swung his hand slightly downward, using wrist action so that his thumb pointed to the front.

"You do that better'n me," Windy said. And then he added, "Almost."

They resumed their whittling, while Gatwin and Harvey watched. It was a brilliant afternoon, the sky cloudless, only a very light wind stirring.

"What you got there?" Windy said suddenly, leaning toward the boy. "Huh—looks like a tree." He chuckled. "Pretty good. A cottonwood tree carved out of cottonwood. Boy, you do pick it all up fast." He spat reflectively, casting a look at the sun, which was moving swiftly down the soft sky.

"You know, the cottonwood, it's a special tree, like I been sayin'. The tribes study everything in nature, and they seen that the least breeze sets the cottonwood leaves to moving, and so they figure it's very sensitive to the Great Spirit. And so a lot of the tribes, they don't burn cottonwood in cookfires. But they use it in their Sun Dance."

He paused. Both of them had been whittling while he talked, and Gatwin and Harvey had just been listening.

Windy reached into his shirt pocket. "See this here cottonwood leaf? You'll see what I mean." He folded the leaf with his big, callused fingers. "See, you fold this edge to edge, like so, and you got the shape of a Sioux tipi."

Zachary had stopped whittling and was staring at the leaf. The man handed it to him. "You keep it. Could be good medicine for you."

Windy picked up his whittling. "Know something else? You take and cut a upper limb of a cottonwood crosswise,

124

and you find you got a five-pointed star; that's a sign of the Great Spirit."

The boy was studying the leaf.

Suddenly a great figure loomed at the edge of the little group of four.

"Private Zachary, you are on stable detail."

The boy looked up, his jaw dropping. Swiftly he jumped to his feet, whipping the cottonwood leaf into his pocket, his other hand saluting.

"No, Goddammit!" roared Ben Cohen. "You do not salute me. I ain't an officer. You salute the lieutenants and the captain." He glared at the boy, his big eyes like a pair of ramrods. "I don't want to have to tell you again. Now get your ass over to the hostler. You got one hell of a lot of shit to shovel."

Young Zachary grabbed up his knife and whittling and broke into a run toward the stable.

"He ain't spoken yet?" said Cohen.

Windy shook his head. "He's gettin' there."

"He's a good kid," Malone said, coming out of the store. "Only thing lacking is he ain't Irish."

"Bullshit!" roared Cohen. "That's what's lacking with you. You keep telling everyone you're Irish, Malone. I think you're faking it." He winked at the others so Malone couldn't see. "In any case, that young feller's got the makin's of a better soldier than any half-dozen of you bums. Now clear out of here. You're using up too much of God's clean fresh air!"

It was dark in the little copse of trees beyond the deadline, but not too dark for the girl to see the anger in Ethan Deal's face. Worse, she could feel it; she could feel the rage coming from his body in great, smothering waves.

She hadn't wanted to come here, but he had insisted. He had threatened her with a beating if she refused. And she knew, since he had already beaten her twice, that even though his body was bent and looked somehow broken, he had tremendous strength. And yet it wasn't his strength that was frightening, it was something else. His . . . will, was it? She wasn't sure, but it was inside him, a force of some kind. And his fits. His fits frightened her. He looked as though he'd had one just recently.

"Goddammit, I told you to get some money. We got no money. How we gonna get out of here and get someplace if we got no money?"

"I don't want to get it like that," Nellie said.

"You don't mind doing it right and left, I notice," he said slyly. "Why give it away free?"

She felt her face color and she was glad it was dark in the trees. "I only did it with that Harvey that time and . . . and with you." she said softly, fighting the tears that came pumping into her eyes and voice.

"Told me you did it with that red devil back at the massacre."

"I didn't. I didn't. He attacked me. I had to, or he would have killed me."

Deal took a step forward. "And now you're too proud to do it with me? Get down on your back."

"I don't want to."

"Don't want to!"

"I don't feel like it. I can't."

"I am telling you, goddammit! You owe me! I saved your lives, you and that brat of a boy. Saved your lives, fed you. and took care of you. Defended you against them red swine when they killed Jessie. Now you by God get down there and get them drawers off!"

She was shaking. "I tell you I can't. I dasn't. I really dasn't. I'm sick. I just can't do it!"

"That's what you said before, and it ain't your time of the month, if that last time you was telling the truth. You do what I say or you'll regret it." He paused to catch his breath, his caved-in chest pumping air. "You done it by God with that sonofabitch you was traveling with who you said was your uncle. That sure wasn't no uncle. Shit! Why, I watched you. Everyone knowed he wasn't your uncle, but your stud horse."

The girl began to back up as he took a step forward, her eyes casting about for some path of escape.

"Don't try callin' the guard," Deal warned her. "I'll kill you. I killed Hester and I can kill you as easy as swattin' a fly."

A sob came strangling out of her throat, and her body began to shake.

"Quiet! Now do as I say. I'll go easy with you, and it won't take too long."

"Last time you hurt me."

She felt rather than saw his grin in the darkening woods. "I know you like it to hurt. I got me a real big one, I have. Hester was always complainin' too. Come on, damn you!"

"Please," she whispered, hardly able to get the word past her trembling lips.

"Dirty little whore!" he snarled, and he reached out to grab her.

"Leave her alone!" The voice was so close behind Deal that they both jumped.

Deal spun around, almost falling as his foot caught a fallen branch. "What the hell!"

"I said you leave her alone!"

"Who in hell—why, it's a soldier boy!"

Private Albert Gatwin stepped farther into the little clearing.

"Mister, how about you just minding your own business!" Deal's head whipped back to the girl. "Or be he another one of your customers?"

"Shut your mouth, you filthy beast!" she snapped suddenly.

A hard laugh cut out of Deal's sneering mouth. "Got a notion to whip your army ass, sonny. Only thing is, I wouldn't want to roust out all them sentries over such a little thing."

"Are you all right, miss?" Gatwin asked the girl.

She was standing very small in front of the two men, holding her hands together at her waist, but they weren't still; the fingers were twisting. Her breath came in uneven spurts, and Gatwin saw her shudder. "I'm... I'm all right."

"You do it with her, sonny, it'll cost you money. And I'll be standing right here watching to see you get your money's worth, and she gets the money."

He was facing Gatwin now, and the sneer on his long face deepened.

Al Gatwin took a breath. He stepped forward. "Get out of here. Get out! Get out, or I'll call the sentry. I'll call him right now."

Deal didn't answer. He seemed to hesitate, his head lowered as though in thought. Then he raised his head, sniffed, hawked, and spat a huge gob of phlegm. Then, slipping his hands under his galluses, without another word, he turned and tromped out of the little clearing.

They stood there silently for some time, and at last Nellie looked up and said, "You followed me."

"I saw you leaving the post and I wanted to talk to you. Didn't know you were meeting him."

"And you heard..."

"Some. Not much." He felt himself coloring. "I tried not to listen. But something in his voice made me feel afraid for you."

They had started to walk out of the wood now, and for a while neither spoke.

The sentry challenged and then passed them, and as they reached the gate, the girl said, "I'm glad you followed."

"So am I."

"It's all right for you to be outside the gate?" she asked.

"I've got a pass. It's all right."

The back of his hand brushed hers, and he felt the shiver go through him. 'My name is Albert Gatwin," he said.

She didn't turn her head to face him, and it was almost totally dark now, but he was sure he saw the smile at the side of her mouth.

"I'm Nellie."

"I know. I'd like to go for a walk with you sometime."

"A walk?" She turned her head toward him now. "I'd like that."

They were right at the gate now, and he wanted to touch her, but then at the same time he knew he didn't. It was a really good moment. It was the first time since he'd run away from home that he didn't feel lonely.

fourteen

The Conways and Mrs. Dodgson had just finished breakfast, and Flora had started to clear the table.

"Most satisfactory," Conway said with a big smile. "I hope you enjoyed it, Mavis." He beamed on his mother-in-law, his mood thoroughly genial. Warner Conway felt in top form.

"Warner, I would like to have a word with you."

Mavis Dodgson, as was her custom, phrased her request as a statement rather than as a question. Her words pulled Conway away from the brightness of his morning, his anticipation of a day of familiar army routine and problems that could be difficult, but over which he felt he could exercise some control.

"Of course, Mavis. But is it something urgent, or can it wait?" He glanced at his watch.

Typically, she ignored the possibility of postponement and simply didn't answer his question, plunging instead right into what she wanted to talk about.

"It's that man Deal. He's spoken to me twice now about his mule and how he's been kept waiting here, just hanging around waiting for the army to decide what it's going to do. Dear Warner, I know you have to follow your routine and all that, but isn't there something that can be done to settle the poor man's problem? I mean, he wants to move on about his business, file his homestead or whatever it is they do—and of course there are the children."

There was no getting a word in until she had said the entire thing, and after two attempts he was finally successful.

"Regiment has been fully informed about the situation of Mr. Deal and his mule. There is nothing more we can do. He wants a horse or payment. The Cheyenne aren't going to give him a horse, and it's up to Regiment to decide about payment. Furthermore, he shot one of the Cheyenne and has almost triggered a good bit of trouble for all of us. So I wouldn't be wasting my sympathy—"

"But they cheated him," she insisted, cutting in. "They told him they'd make a trade, and then they simply tried to steal both his mules."

"Mavis, first of all, the mule was dead before it was shot."

"That isn't what Mr. Deal says."

"I'm sure it isn't." Conway felt his ire rising, and even Flora, smiling at him from the doorway, didn't help.

"And those two children. The boy should be in school. More than that, he should be receiving medical attention for his speech, or lack of it. He definitely has something the matter with him, and it should be taken care of. As for the girl—"

"Mavis, Mavis, slow down a minute—please!"

"Slow down, Warner? But you must do something about that young girl. She's . . . she's wild. Mr. Deal had

132

a great deal to say about that young...thing."

"I'm sure he did," Conway said, forcing himself to be calm. "But why do you believe all that?"

"He knows her. He had some pretty hard things to say, some pretty hard things! Oh, Warner, you know where there's smoke, there's fire."

"I think she's rather a fine young lady."

"Look at her!" Mrs. Dodgson protested. "A child. All the men ogling, and her setting her cap for them. Really! I mean really, Warner!" She shook herself, as ruffled as a brood hen disturbed in the performance of her natural duty. "It's no wonder the poor man has had his fits aggravated."

Conway had been about to excuse himself and escape to his office, when her words stopped him. "Fits? What fits?"

Mavis Dodgson regarded her son-in-law in utter puzzlement. "You don't know about his fits? Why, don't you know he's a sick man? That is what I've been trying to get across to you. He needs to get out of here, get his homestead or whatever, but he can't without his horse. This whole affair has made his condition much worse."

Conway looked over at Flora, who had just finished with the dishes. "Did you know anything about Deal's fits?"

"Nothing," she said. "Although he certainly looks anything but healthy."

Flora looked at her mother, who was standing in the middle of the room, her hand raised in disbelief to the side of her face, her mouth round with surprise and outrage at the callousness of the army and her son-in-law.

Later, in his office, Conway asked Matt Kincaid the same question he'd asked Flora. "Do you know anything about Deal having fits?"

"Not a thing, sir."

"Does Windy?"

"I'm pretty sure he doesn't, or he would have said so."

"Apparently—according to Mrs. Dodgson—he's been suffering from some malady most of his life. That's why his body is caved in the way it is. He fell off a hay wagon and broke his spine and shoulders when he was quite young."

"During a fit, sir?"

"That is what he told Mrs. Dodgson." Conway's lips tightened. "She is also on the warpath about Nellie and Zack. Says they ought to be in a decent home, in school and so on. Which is true."

"That certainly is true, sir. Nobody could argue with that. But it seems to me the most important thing is to get them away from Deal."

Conway was nodding vigorously even before Kincaid had finished.

"He's more or less given up on the boy," Matt went on. "Zack has attached himself to Windy and some of the other men, but he's mostly glued to our fine scout, sir."

"I am happy about that," Conway said, slapping the top of his desk. "I'm damn happy about that."

"But Nellie is another matter, Captain. I've gathered that Deal sticks pretty close to her. I have a sneaking suspicion that Mr. Deal is, uh..."

"More friendly than necessary?" Conway said. "Or at any rate, wishes to be? Is that it?"

"That's it, sir."

"Ben Cohen was telling me the same thing yesterday." Conway shifted in his chair. "Matt, we've got all kinds of loose ends here. Now what about Deal's horse? As I see it, it's a standoff. They're not giving him a horse, and he sure can't engage in a knife fight with one of those young warriors, or even with one of the old ones; and Regiment, you know, will not pay him for a horse or a mule, or even for a tick! So where does that leave us? I mean, I just don't see any way out."

"Not if we want to maintain friendly relations with the Cheyenne, sir."

"They're pretty damn mad about the squatters on their doorstep, aren't they?"

"I've a notion the Jellicoes aren't planning to stay out on that doorstep too long, sir."

"Matt, we've gotten in more information on Jellicoe. Nothing we didn't know already, but it puts a little more meat on the bones." Conway ran his hand along the side of his jaw, realizing he had missed a couple of places when shaving. "The thing is, we don't want the Jellicoes around here. We know, though we can't prove it, that Jellicoe and his boys pulled the raid on the McCone wagon train. And we know he'll be planning more. Now you know how thin we're spread with the territory we have to cover. He could become a real problem. Old brigands don't change their spots, they just get more vicious."

"I fully agree, sir. But we can't exactly order him out unless we catch him redhanded at something. He is on federal land, and since we've allowed other squatters into the territory, we don't want to look as though we're picking on Jellicoe."

"Exactly. And of course it would help if Washington could be a little more decisive about the situation. But that's an old, old story." Conway sighed. He leaned back in his chair and ran his fingers through his hair. "Any ideas, Lieutenant?"

Kincaid said, "Jellicoe picked his own time and his own place when he hit the McCone train. There were six of them, though they're vicious enough to take on double their own number. But still, the wagon train could have handled it if Jellicoe hadn't been smart. The way he got them off guard is what I mean."

Conway nodded.

"I'd feel pretty safe in betting that he'll be calling in extra help for his next one," Matt said. "He won't take a chance on trying the soldier trick twice."

"You mean he'll start bringing gunmen into the territory?"

"Sir, you know he's calling his place Jellicoe City. Kind of a joke. But not so funny. If he can get away with it, he'll put up a couple of buildings—a saloon, a livery, and such—and the next thing you know, we'll have a gun-and-gambling town right in the middle of the territory, right on the toes of the Cheyenne, not to mention the Sioux."

"Pretty as a picture," Conway said sardonically. "I'm still asking for ideas, Matt."

"I know, sir. I'd like to talk it over with Windy. I know there's something here; it's just a question of seeing it."

"It's a question of seeing it soon enough," said Conway. He picked up a paper from his desk. "This is the latest dispatch from Regiment. There's a big wagon train due. Should be reaching Riley's Crossing within the week."

When there came a knock on the door, Conway said, "That could be Deal. I asked Ben Cohen to get him over here so we could at least try to get settled on his situation."

But it wasn't Ethan Deal. It was Ben Cohen.

"Sir," he said, "Mr. Deal is not in his quarters. It doesn't look like his bed has been slept in. I've sent men looking for him, sir, but I'm pretty sure he's left the post."

"Thank you, Sergeant. I want the post searched with

a fine-toothed comb. And Tipi Town. What about the boy and girl?"

"They're here, sir."

When the door had closed behind the first sergeant, Conway reached for his cigars. "Well, Matt, as I said, we've got less than a week. Maybe only a couple of days."

"By God, Paw, she is a big one." It was Porter Jellicoe speaking as they sat around the table in the sod house.

The evening meal had been completed, and coffee, whiskey, and cards were in evidence. The room stank of tobacco and grease, whiskey and sweat, and coal oil from the two lamps.

"It'll be the biggest yet," Purvis Jellicoe said proudly. "I whistled up some extra help, just to make sure. With the Hendry boys siding us, we shouldn't have no trouble."

They grinned in anticipation of the rewards that would come to them.

"Then, after, we'll lay low. We'll be good ol' honest citizens, growing stuff, helping the country, all that."

"But, Paw," Poon said suddenly, as a thought struck him. "If we got more people workin' with us, we got more people to split with."

A grim silence filled the soddy as Poon's trenchant observation struck down their high spirits.

"Shit," said Print, and looked at the old man.

Purvis Jellicoe drank, holding the neck of the bottle to his loose lips. Gasping, he placed the whiskey on the table. He surveyed his offspring as he bit off a chunk of cut-plug and began slowly working it in his sharp yellow teeth.

"Boy," he muttered, his jaws going as fast as a prairie dog's. "Boy, I sure got me some assholes for sons."

The boys were long used to these parental observa-

137

tions, which were frequent and also loud. But perhaps it was the burden of such a family that kept Purvis so frisky.

"I am sometimes wondering if you be a real son of mine, Palmer or Poon or whatever the hell your name is. Seems to me sometimes the stork delivered to the wrong place. I just can't figger why you are so dumb!"

The old man reached again for the bottle, his eyes sweeping the circle of faces. He drank, greedily and almost choking, but not losing a drop.

The Jellicoe sons watched the sly grin sneaking onto their sire's face, and now a streak of laughter ran through the group as the old man, his eyebrows raised like those of a teacher waiting for his pupils who were just an inch away from revelation, started to shake. His throat quivered, a little bark bounced out of his mouth, his eyes closed; and now the others, traveling right with him, picked it up, and all at once the soddy was rocking with their laughter. They roared, tears springing from their eyes as they gasped for air. Porter fell off his seat, and Prior collapsed on top of the table, while Print laughed so hard his side hurt him and he didn't know whether he was laughing or had broken a rib or two. Just the *thought* of sharing with the Hendry boys was the funniest thing they'd ever come across.

Poon fell across Prior, almost collapsing the table, while the author of all the amusement, the old man, slid to the dirt floor and lay on his back, staring at the roof while his body shook soundlessly.

Old Man Jellicoe lay there speaking to the sod roof. "Didn't ride with Quantrill without learnin' somethin', be it known! Hell, if money ain't just the same as gold dust."

"How you mean that, Paw?" somebody asked. "Always thought gold was money anyways."

"Well, see, you got some gold dust here, see," said Purvis, continuing to lie on his back and directing his words to the roof of the soddy. "And then like you got these figures you want to cover with the gold dust. Like them statues we seen that time in Kansas City. Howsomever, if you got too little gold, you cannot cover all them figures. No matter how you slice it, you cannot cover. So what do you do then? Eh? What do you do?"

A stunned silence fell on his listeners. It was always a dreadful moment when Paw asked questions like that, for they all knew the trap behind the bait.

This time Poon was brave. "Why, shit, Paw, you got to get rid of some of the figures."

Paw Jellicoe, still on his back, suddenly let out a great yahoo of a yell. "By jingo, you got it, boy! You got it! We get rid of *all* them figures, boy. *All!*"

And now they began to hoot with laughter and give out the rebel yell, and finally Porter whipped out his Deane & Adams, which he'd taken off one of the bodies at the wagon train, and fired three fast shots into the roof.

The old man, lying on his back, was almost strangling. He gargled, hawked, then spat, getting most of it in his beard. His eyes squeezed out more tears. And at last he lay there, his breath sawing in great gasps.

Silence fell. Many moments passed, and the silence was broken only by the snoring of some of the soddy's occupants.

Suddenly the old man sat up like a spring.

"Rider," he said, getting swiftly to his feet and kicking one of the snorers. "Get your asses moving. We got company."

He was all business as he stepped to the door of the soddy and peered through a little porthole just next to it.

"One horsebacker," he said.

Now, stumbling out of their sleep, they heard the

horse nicker, and a man's voice calling out.

Paw held up his hand for quiet. In his other hand he gripped his big Navy Colt. He stepped away from the door, and signaling with his left hand, he placed the Jellicoes strategically about the soddy.

Then he blew out one lamp, removed its chimney and wick, and carried it to the side of the door, where he held it so that he could throw the coal oil on the visitor if necessary.

Reaching over, he unlatched the door.

"Come on in, mister. Door's open."

The six Jellicoes watched the door push open, and a tall, dark figure entered, stooping to make it beneath the door frame.

"Porter, Print." The old man motioned with his gun for them to see whether it was all clear outside; and they moved past the tall visitor.

"Come on in, stranger. Be you a preacher man?" Purvis Jellicoe chuckled. "Then you'll have a drink with the Jellicoes."

"I am a man of God," Ethan Deal said, "and I am sure tuckered out. I will join you in some strong libation with gratitude, sir."

Matt Kincaid had just walked past the stable at about ten o'clock at night when he thought he heard a strange bird calling from near the doorway. He stopped, listening. But then the unevenness of the sound made him realize it was someone crying.

"What are you doing here?" he said, coming upon the huddled figure, which was almost indistinguishable from the side of the building.

It was Nellie who turned her pale, tear-streaked face toward him.

"I am sorry, Lieutenant. I . . . I'm sorry."

"Come," he said kindly. "Walk with me. I'm making my rounds, but we can talk. And we might even have a cup of coffee."

She had risen and was facing him now, but with her head down, now and again wiping at her eyes with the back of her wrist.

"I don't want to be seen like this."

"Come on, it's a nice night for a walk. No one will see you."

They crossed the parade, then mounted the parapet at the gate. Al Gatwin was on tower duty and saluted smartly as Lieutenant Kincaid and Nellie approached, forcing his eyes away from Nellie, who was staring at him. Gatwin couldn't resist, however, and when the lieutenant had turned away, he stole a glance at the girl, who was watching him with her head bent, though he could discern the tiny smile at the corners of her lips. When she raised her eyes to his and fluttered her fingers at him, he thought he would dissolve with happiness.

Then, turning to follow Kincaid, she started to cry again.

"How about some coffee, or maybe tea," Matt said gently as they approached the mess hall.

"That would be nice, sir. Thank you. Tea would be nice."

In a few moments they were in Matt's office with a pot of tea.

"Now tell me what's the problem," he said.

She had stopped crying, and her eyes were almost dry. "It's Deal."

"I've sent someone to track him, but we've had no news yet. Tell me what you know about his disappearing."

She shrugged. "I can't say much. You know his room is close to where I am with Zachary. Well, last night, in the middle of the night, I heard this crash. I thought right away he was having one of his fits. He falls down usually."

"Until this morning I never knew he had fits," Matt said.

"He has them often. And sometimes he gets pretty bad, thrashing around, foaming at the mouth, even. It's real scary. It really scares Zachary. And me too."

Matt took a drink of his tea. "Just what sort of fits are they?"

"I don't know. He doesn't say. Maybe he doesn't know himself just what they are. But they're awful. He jerks around and rolls and cries out sometimes."

"So what happened? You heard this crash..."

"First I made sure Zachary was asleep. Then I went to Deal's room. His door wasn't locked. He was lying on the floor. His eyes were staring, like they do. He was over the attack, I guess. I mean, he wasn't having any convulsions, and he was breathing all right. The lamp was lit and he just lay there, sweating a lot. He was all wet and staring up at the ceiling and breathing heavy."

"Did he speak? Did he say something?"

"Not right away. I asked him did he want anything, like maybe some water, but he didn't answer." She sniffed, and rubbed her nose with the back of her hand. "Then he started to talk in a little while."

"What did he say?"

"Told me he was going to get his horse that was owed him and get out of here. Said he wanted me to come with him."

"And Zachary?"

She shook her head. "No, he'd been talking to me before about coming with him and I'd been telling him no, I didn't want to."

"And you told him that now?"

She nodded her head, her fingers twisting together in

her lap. "He said he'd kill me if I didn't come."

Matt stared at her. "He actually said he'd kill you?"

"He's said that before. Only this time I knew it was different." She looked at Matt directly for the first time since she'd been speaking. "I was scared. I *am* scared, Lieutenant Kincaid."

"Why didn't you tell somebody about it?"

"I was afraid. He'd already told me he killed his wife and he'd just as soon kill me."

"But nobody believes he killed his wife, Nellie. He might have thought he did. That kind of thing happens to people sometimes when they've been in a massacre. And if he was having those fits—well, he was a sick man already."

The girl had been sitting close to him and now she reached forward and touched his arm. "Lieutenant, I know he killed his wife."

"How do you know that? Did you see him?"

"He told me he killed her."

"He told me the same thing, but I'm sure he didn't."

"Yes, but...he also told me how he'd confessed it to everyone, and that nobody believed him because they thought he was all upset because of the Indian attack. But he made up the story. He said it like that just so people wouldn't believe him."

Matt looked at her incredulously. "You mean he actually came to after the fight, found his wife alive, and killed her?"

The girl nodded.

"And then he confessed it in such a way that we would be sure not to believe him. Is that what you're saying, Nellie?"

"That's exactly what he told me, Lieutenant."

"Did he say why he killed her? He must have had some reason."

"He said because she was always mocking him about

his fits. Saying he wasn't a real man, that he was weak, crazy, out of his mind. He said she tormented him into it; and when he saw the opportunity right after the fighting, he just picked up a singletree and hit her."

"A singletree!"

"That's what he said." Nellie looked him right in the eye as she said, "But he told you he hit her with his rifle, didn't he?"

"He told you he said that, eh?"

She nodded. "Because he said the Indians don't leave any weapons lying around after a raid, and you know that and so wouldn't believe his story, that he'd killed his wife."

Kincaid said nothing for a long moment; he was remembering how both he and Conway, and Windy too, had not believed Deal's confession. And now he knew why.

"So you be lookin' for the Cheyenne camp, eh?" It was Purvis Jellicoe speaking—leaning back, snapping his single suspender, scratching his crotch, rooting in his armpits and his nose; spitting, hawking, belching, and farting, roaring with laughter as he and his sons guzzled whiskey and surveyed their visitor.

"Well, Yankee preacher, you don't mind separating yourself from your hair, then," Palmer said.

"Supposed to be at peace," Deal said. "All I am after is justice. They owe me a horse, and by God"—he patted his ancient muzzle-loading rifle—"and by God that horse will be forthcomin'. I speak, sir, as a man of God; and I vow to wreak holiest vengeance on them red heathen, should they attempt to keep me from my purpose."

"To get yer hoss..." Prior grinned, his jaw jutting forward, his little eyes alight, while Palmer's tongue showed just the tip through his lips.

"And to get me some homesteading land. I been told

the land is here for the taking."

"What fool told you that?" Old Man Jellicoe demanded.

"The Lord told me that!"

"Who?"

"The Lord, goddammit! The Lord told me! I was walking along a road back in William Falls and I heard the voice calling me. I stopped and asked for guidance and the voice of the Lord came clear as a bell. 'Go to the West,' it said." Ethan Deal had closed both his eyes as he said those words, and now they sprang wide open. "This I am doing." He paused, frowning. "Ethan Deal is doing the Lord's work."

"Well, Yankee preacher, we maybe could use a sharp, singleminded feller like yourself," said Porter Jellicoe, his long face sliced all the way across in a grin.

"Use me, hah!" Deal's eyes glittered at the bottle on the table. "I could surely use a mite of that there liquid to still my shaking."

The men burst into a roar. They loved it. Poon poured him an enormous glass of whiskey.

Old Man Jellicoe leaned forward, his little eyes popping out of their sockets like stones. "Preacher," he began, all innocence, "you been visiting down by the soldier boy's camp. What you hear around there? What they up to?"

"Supposed to be up to replacing my mule Jessie. But they ain't doin' nothin'. It's why I'm getting that horse myself, like I just got through telling you, mister."

"They patrolling around these here parts?" Print asked.

"I dunno. I don't give nary a thought to them soldiers, all the time runnin' about, salutin' and kissin' ass."

They rocked with laughter. Prior almost capsized the bottle of whiskey, slapping the table, but fortunately Poon saved it.

"What they do for pussy in that place is what I want

to know," Print said. "All men and hardly a woman about."

"They do it with each other," Porter said.

"Yup," said Palmer. "They make a big circle in their parade ground and each other does it to the next one, all in one big circle!"

"Captain's got his wife," Deal said when the laughter had subsided. "And the first sergeant, he has got his wife too. The rest—I dunno. Of course, there is the squaws over to Tipi Town."

"What the hell is Tipi Town?"

"The Indian village where the friendlies—that's what *they* call 'em—stay. I hear there is a lot of fornicatin' there." His eyes rolled toward the roof of the soddy. "Ah, the Lord will hand them their just desserts, you can be sure. Them soldiers is idle, and any clean, honest man knows that idleness is the shipwreck of chastity."

"It is what?" shouted Porter. "Idleness is what?"

"I will tell you yet another sayin' on it." Deal held his forefinger high. "'Idleness is a house out of which all sins come.'"

"Say, preacher, what'll you do if, when you walk into the Injun camp lookin' for that horse, they just up and scalp your ass right now?" said Palmer Jellicoe, giggling.

"I will just tell them I want the horse they promised me. My cause is just. The Lord will protect me!"

Suddenly Purvis Jellicoe leaned forward onto the table, placing his big forearm there and drumming his fingers on the tabletop. "Say, preacher, you got some money?"

"Money?"

"Yeah, that's what I said." The old man looked around at his boys, who had sobered suddenly.

"Don't have no money. I am a poor man of the Lord."

"But you been drinkin' our whiskey now. How you figure to pay for that?"

146

Ethan Deal had indeed consumed a good amount of the Jellicoe whiskey, as he noticed when he pushed himself to his feet.

"Think you better pay us some money," the old man said.

But Ethan Deal didn't hear him. His head felt suddenly thick, and at the same time empty. There was a buzzing in his ears, and a great shudder ran through him as, before his eyes, the whole room lighted up. For an unendurable second everything in the whole world was still and immaculate. And then, with a cry, he fell to the floor.

"Holy shit!" said Purvis Jellicoe. "What the fuck is going on!"

Deal was thrashing about on the dirt floor, saliva frothing out of his mouth, while his body seemed to be twisting into knots. Another cry tore from his throat; then suddenly he lay still.

After a moment one of the boys asked, "Is he dead?"

"He's still breathin'."

"Yeah—but funny-like."

"Jesus," someone said, "where in the hell did he come from?"

"Don't know where he come from," answered the old man. "But we sure know where he is goin'."

fifteen _____

"Looks to me like we're about to be gettin' ourselves a permanent preacher here at Jellicoe City!"

Ethan Deal had suddenly focused his eyes on the dark
round hole of Purvis Jellicoe's gunbarrel, which was just
inches away from his forehead. Behind it was the grinning, bearded face of the patriarch of the Jellicoe clan.

Deal felt the ice in his veins. "You help me get my
horse, I will tell you some more news from the army
camp." He stammered the words, for he was not at all
comfortable, lying on his back on the ground with that
big .45 right there, waiting to blow his head off.

"That is bullshit, Paw," said Poon Jellicoe. "But, shit,
don't blow the old boy's brains out in here. It'll make
one fucking mess."

"Wait a minute now. You rascals just wait a minute!"
The grinning face leaned closer to Deal, the gunbarrel
almost touching him. "What news? Eh? What news you
got?"

"Somethin' you didn't know, I bet. They got the whole of the second platoon out to some place called Crazy Woman Creek."

Old Man Jellicoe jerked his eyes up toward Prior and Poon, who were standing over Deal. "That's up by the Bozeman, ain't it?"

"Right, Paw."

"And," said the old man, "that is where that other wagon train is s'posed to be coming in—the one we talked about—'fore it hits the Bozeman."

"Gee, Paw, that is right."

"Could be this asshole here mowt be tellin' it straight." Purvis sat back on his heels, and with a sudden fast belch he stood up. "Get up," he said. "Set on that there box." He pointed with the .45. "What else you heard?"

"Heard there was a wagon train the platoon was gonna escort."

"That one? That one at Crazy Woman Creek?"

Deal nodded, his eyes darting among the members of the Jellicoe family who clustered in a semicircle at the table. "And there is another train coming through a place called Hogshead Butte."

"You sure about that?"

"I am telling you, sure."

"'Cause if you are fibbin'..." The old man purred the words. "If you are fibbin' me, I won't kill you, preacher. Oh, no. That wouldn't be what I'd do. Me an' the boys will stake you out. You know what a anthill stakeout is, Yankee preacher?"

"I heard of them."

"Then be careful."

"I am telling you the Lord's truth. All I want is my horse. Now I have given you the information. Just give me a horse and let me go."

"We will let you go when we see it's not lies you been telling us."

"Paw, I don't get it," said Porter. "Where the hell is this Crazy Woman Creek in our plan? What's that got to do with our haul with the Hendry boys? And what's this Hogshead Butte?"

"Dumb asshole," growled the old man, holstering his Navy Colt. "This here with the Hendry bunch is at Riley's Crossing. But the army will be down waiting at Hogshead Butte, while we hit 'em at Riley's. The other, at Crazy Woman Creek, that's north of here. But the army's got to protect them, too. See? So they will be weakened." He swung back to Deal. "They sent a whole platoon?"

"That's right."

"But Paw," said Print. "How you know he's tellin' it straight? The sonofabitch could still be lying."

"Jesus," said Purvis Jellicoe. The word was soft, falling like a little ball of velvet on a blanket. The old man's patience was exquisite. "Boys, listen to me just one time. Why you think I planned this whole thing? I *knowed* already the army was sending a bunch of soldiers to escort some other wagon train. Just didn't know for sure where and how many. You think I am dumb enough to take on the whole fucking outpost down there with just us?" He paused, his breath sawing. "That's why I got holt of Hendry. But even then we need all the advantage we can get. It's one thing to deal with maybe a platoon of them soldiers, but two or three is foolishness. Just foolishness." He paused, rooting at his buttocks with his left hand. "They got to keep one platoon at the post for protection, then they got one at Crazy Woman Creek, and that leaves one at the most for here at Riley's Crossing. Jesus Christ, I am sure tired of having to explain everything all the time to you boys!" He spat suddenly and very fast at the floor. "I got it underlined now," he said, "with the preacher's telling us what I already knowed." He paused again. "Sure, we could do it without Hendry, but it's better to have a sure thing."

151

Suddenly he whipped out the .45. "All right, preacher. You told it straight. But you keep straight with me, or you are gonna for sure end up with your permanent residence in Jellicoe City."

"What about my horse?"

"Fuck your horse!"

Suddenly the door of the soddy opened and Palmer stepped in. "Horses," he said.

"Army?"

"It ain't the army and it ain't the fucking Indians."

"Then it'll be Hendry and his boys," the old man said, and there was a big grin on his grizzled face.

The two riders had drawn rein at the top of the coulee, and now, protected by the box elders, they were looking down on the sod hut.

"I tracked him to here," Windy said. "If Deal's still alive, he is in there."

"What makes you think he might not be alive?" Matt Kincaid asked, holding his eyes on the soddy below.

"He is such a blowhard, he just might rile those Jellicoes, who are more often than not on a hair trigger, I believe. And you seen what they done at Jack Creek."

Kincaid felt a tightening inside himself as the scene of the massacre swept into his mind.

"I wouldn't recommend you and me riding down there and asking for the man, even though you are an officer in the United States Army." And Windy nodded in the direction of the circular corral, in which were quite a few head of horses. "Looks like they have got some company."

"That doesn't look so good," Matt said slowly. "It'll mean they're getting extra help to attack the wagon train at Riley's Crossing."

"Well, like the captain says, we have got no time, but

we do have a hell of a big one to pull out of the fire."
Windy slipped his right foot out of its stirrup and scratched
the back of his thigh. "They surely know all about the
wagon train, and they more than likely know how shorthanded we are." Windy nodded his head off to the north-
west. "And we got that explaining to do to Faraway Eagle
if we don't want that whole Cheyenne tribe on our asses."

Kincaid watched Windy's Adam's apple pump up and
down a couple of times, and for a moment he wondered
if the scout had swallowed his cut-plug.

"Shit, we are spread too damn thin," Windy grinned.
"But that's the way we like it, ain't it?" Slipping his foot
back into its stirrup, he turned his pony's head. "What
are we going to do about Running Bull?" he said as he
rode alongside Matt. "You got any answers?"

"I might."

Windy cut a glance at Kincaid for a clue. "I got one
guess. You are expecting your friend, the noble scout of
Easy Company, to engage in this knife fight with Buffalo
Shirt or whoever else they might pick because Deal has
gone north, south, east, or maybe even west; and anyways, he is in no shape to face a young man with a sharp
knife. So the honor of the Cheyenne and the Contraries,
as well as the honor of the United States Army, will be
saved."

"Wrong."

Windy's head whipped around to look at Kincaid in
some surprise. Matt had raised the gait of his horse, and
Windy's roan had to step fast to match it.

"Matt, old friend, I hope you are not thinking of doing
what I think you're thinking of doing."

"Only I am not thinking about it, my friend."

"You've never been in a knife fight."

"Until the first time I got laid, I'd never been laid."

"Ain't the same."

"Whatever, it's the way it's going to be. Faraway Eagle and those ornery Contraries have got to be satisfied, or we are in more trouble than we can handle."

"Conway know about this?"

They were cantering across a long, flat stretch of ground, and Matt turned his head toward the scout. "Let me put it this way," he said. "He will."

"Seems worse than the last time," Matt said to Windy as they rode into the Cheyenne camp.

"Wait," the scout replied. "Things can always get worse."

Dismounting in stony silence, they were greeted by Faraway Eagle.

"First we will smoke," the chief said. "And then we will talk of Running Bull and the white man." He was wearing a white man's broad-brimmed hat with a single eagle feather sticking up from it.

They sat with the chief and his headmen and some of the Contraries in a grove of cottonwoods not far from the chief's lodge. It was quiet and peaceful, without the heavy feeling of anger that there had been when they first rode in.

Through an opening in the trees, Matt watched the soft movement of goldenrod and blue asters as the wind stirred, blowing the strong horse-smell of the pony herd toward him.

At last they had finished with the long pipe, and Faraway Eagle said, "We must speak now of Running Bull and the man of the mule."

"The mule man has run away," Matt said. "But he was too old and ill to fight anyway."

Faraway Eagle accepted this in silence and then he spoke in Cheyenne to his headmen and the Contraries, only some of whom understood English. When he had finished, there was much muttering.

"You know that this must be settled now," Faraway
Eagle said to the two white men. "Our young men are
restless, and with so many white men coming, it is hard
to control them. But the honor of the Dog Soldier Society
is at stake here."

"The army agrees with that, Faraway Eagle. And so
I wish to fight Buffalo Shirt if he is still willing to fight
in his brother's place."

His words were followed by a tight silence that lasted
for some moments. Matt looked at the faces of the Cheyenne, especially that of Faraway Eagle. The chief's face
was stern, as it almost always was in council with the
whites, yet it was not hard; Matt realized there was a
kind of mobility behind the tremendous stillness of his
expression.

Finally Faraway Eagle spoke in Cheyenne, following
which there was much talk among the Contraries and the
headmen. Matt and Windy simply waited.

At length, Faraway Eagle raised his hand and the
group was again quiet.

"It is well," he said. "You have chosen the good way,
Lieutenant. Buffalo Shirt will meet you with the knives."

Stripped to the waist, they were both lean and sinewy,
their bodies still within their control, still theirs, not
having yet reached those years when the life-energy ran
just a bit slower, the blood a bit thicker. The Cheyenne,
however, had a few years' advantage over Kincaid. Buffalo Shirt was in his twenties, and while Matt was in
sharp condition, ten years' difference had to be reckoned
with. Moreover, Kincaid was inexperienced with knives.

Now there was a brief discussion among the Contraries
as to how Buffalo Shirt would fight. Would he fight
Kincaid as a Contrary, or in the regular way of the warrior? The Indian had been standing crouched before Matt
with his big skinning knife in his right hand, but now,

at a word from Faraway Eagle, he shifted it to his left, and at the same time exchanged his feet, so that his stance, too, was altered.

At another word from Faraway Eagle, the combatants advanced toward each other and began circling.

The tribe had gathered in a meadow not far from the camp, forming a circle around the two opponents. It was hot, the sun bearing down on their bare backs, but neither felt it.

"I not fight you, my friend," Buffalo Shirt said, and smiled, instantly striking at Kincaid.

Matt barely dodged the flashing blade.

"I kill you now," the Contrary said, moving away.

Kincaid followed warily, sweeping his blade across from left to right. A murmur rose from the spectators at the sight of the little red thread of blood on Buffalo Shirt's forearm.

Buffalo Shirt cried out, "Oh, I am dying!" And he staggered, his arm hanging limp, while Matt watched him warily.

All at once the Indian sprang forward, and now there was a loud murmur as the tip of his blade caught Kincaid on the upper arm. Fortunately Matt had been moving away, and the wound was superficial.

Now Buffalo Shirt darted in and immediately sprang back; and again he feinted, ducked, bobbed, and weaved. Kincaid circled so that he was always facing the Indian.

Again Buffalo Shirt struck with his blade, waist high, and Matt felt the point of the knife strike along the top of his trousers. Swiftly he slashed at the Indian's shoulder and saw the thin pencil line of blood.

Buffalo Shirt screamed, clutching his shoulder, his face contorted in agony. Matt drove in and their knife arms locked in midair. At the same time Buffalo Shirt grabbed Kincaid around the waist in a bear hug, while Matt's free arm circled the Indian's neck. Locked together, they kept their feet, struggling for advantage. Suddenly Kincaid kicked his heel against Buffalo Shirt's ankle, and they were on the ground; but still together, neither one letting go his grip as they rolled in the grass.

"We fight to death," Buffalo Shirt said in Matt's ear. "We each not wound each other, so we not stop fighting."

Suddenly Buffalo Shirt sank his teeth into Kincaid's neck, and when the white man loosened his hold, the Indian broke free. Rolling swiftly across the clearing, he was up on his feet in a flash. But Matt was right with him; and once again they circled each other.

"Do what he tells you, Matt," Windy called. "Listen to what he's telling you."

Throwing a quick glance in the direction of the scout, Matt saw that Windy was standing huddled with some of the Contraries, including Buffalo Shirt's wounded brother, Running Bull.

"We fight to death," Buffalo Shirt said again. "We each not wound each other, so we not stop fighting." And he slashed again with his knife, missing his opponent.

"Do what he's telling you, Matt!" Windy called out again. "Just remember he's speaking ass backwards."

Kincaid ran his forearm across his face to get the sweat out of his eyes, and continued to watch the Indian. He thought he detected something like a smile in Buffalo Shirt's eyes, but he knew he'd better not fool himself.

Then Buffalo Shirt said, "I kill, you kill—both dead. I wound, you wound—both wound." He stretched out his arms in front of him. "Me best warrior; but I kill you and you kill me. We not settle fight by dropping knives. Honor is not cleaned. Two cowards fight, is the same as great warriors." He sprang forward and nicked Matt once again, but this time on his other arm.

"Now you not wound me," he said. "You kill, not wound me."

157

He slid toward Matt, who, praying he was doing the right thing when he saw the opening that could allow the ultimate cut, instead struck lightly, drawing another thin red line of blood. Each had been wounded three times.

Buffalo Shirt threw down his knife.

"It's a draw!" shouted Windy.

Matt threw his knife on top of Buffalo Shirt's.

"It is enough," Faraway Eagle said. "It is good. The Contrary Ones are satisfied."

Buffalo Shirt was grinning. "You bad man, you coward," he said, offering his hand to Matt.

"I hate you," Matt said, grinning as he shook the Contrary's hand vigorously.

Windy walked up and handed Matt his tunic.

"Faraway Eagle has invited us to dinner," he said. "Looks like you really pulled a good one out of the hat, old boy."

One of the Contraries came over. It was Running Bull. He was limping slightly.

"You hot? You want water?"

"Yes—I do."

Smiling, Running Bull handed him a cup filled with sand.

"No," said Matt, catching on fast. "I want some sand."

But the meal with Faraway and his headmen and the Contraries was served straight. It had been cooked by the chief's youngest wife, Falling Leaf. Afterwards the Contraries showed their "fooling around" to the entire camp.

The young man was slender, supple as a whip, and he made the white men and the True People laugh with his bizarre antics and peculiar clothes. Walking backward, holding the soldier hat over his face, with the back of his head where his face should be, he never faltered;

he knew exactly what he was doing.

In backward pantomime he fought an enemy, shooting himself with imaginary arrows, and escaping from the foe, plunging into a creek and swimming across it, his body arched on the ground, sweeping the dust behind him as he actually "swam" the little clearing, his body moving as swiftly as though he were actually in the water.

Now more of the Contraries plunged into the "water," splashing one another, singing and laughing, spouting imaginary water from their mouths, and, like the first one, actually swimming along the ground.

Matt and Windy laughed harder than anybody. And the mood that had shut them out when they first rode into camp had dissolved completely.

Yes, for a moment the People were again happy, Faraway Eagle saw. It was good to see these things done backwards, the foolishness lifting their spirits, reminding them of the smallness, the impermanence of their lives and, by contrast, the greatness of the Above.

When Matt and Windy rode away from the camp it was late afternoon.

Windy said, "See, they only wanted it to set right with their rules, their honor. They liked it that you wanted to fight in Deal's place. So they figured that was the way to settle it. And it was. It was good."

"But I didn't want to fight him," Matt said with a sly grin as he looked at the scout.

"Shit," said Windy. "We better get out of here fast, before you catch that craziness."

"No—I want to stay," Matt said. Drawing rein, he stopped his bay horse and then began walking him backwards.

Suddenly he stopped, and his face was serious again. "Know something, Windy? I think I've got a real crazy idea. But it's a crazy idea that might just be what the doctor ordered." He had turned his horse.

"You really are heading back there, eh? Now I know you've gone loco."

"Come on, old scout, we need another talk with Faraway Eagle."

sixteen _____

"What the hell you think you're doing? Blowing that bugle out your ass?" demanded a furious Ben Cohen. "This is an army post, soldier, not a fucking ladies' home society!"

Reb McBride's color changed at least three times during the first sergeant's outburst.

"Sarge, I was just trying to get some melody into it—"

"Melody . . ." Ben Cohen's large eyes rolled back into his head, as though he had given up the ghost. "Melody . . ." He barely breathed the word. Finally those hard eyes leveled on Easy Company's bugler. "Corporal McBride, you are not this company's bugler in order to get melody or music or any other goddamn thing out of that bugle. Your job is to blow reveille and whatever else your orders call for. Now, goddammit, stop blowing that thing like it was a violin!" He glared furiously at the wretched McBride. "Don't tell me," he said, holding up his hand and turning his huge head to one side. "Do not

161

tell me whose suggestion it was you were following."

"But, Sarge—"

"But nothing!"

"Sarge, Mrs. Dodg—"

"Soldier, reveille ain't supposed to sound good! It's supposed to wake these bums up, not lull them into sweet dreams! When I tell you to blow reveille, you goddamn well blow *reveille!*"

In his office, Captain Warner Conway sat looking at his second-in-command. "The point," he was saying, "is not just to get these emigrants through on their way west, or to handle those who are trying to settle around the territory; the point right now"—and his middle finger drove into the top of his desk—"is to get rid of Jellicoe and his boys." He paused, lacing his fingers together as he leaned forward in emphasis. "We know damn well it was the Jellicoes who wiped out the wagons at Jack Creek. I'd bet a year's pay on that, even though we can't prove it in Regiment's eyes." He paused. "Now we've got the whole of Second Platoon up at Crazy Woman Creek, so it's not likely Jellicoe will hit there. Besides, it's pretty far away."

"Sir, I'm certain, and so is Windy, that they'll be aiming at Riley's Crossing. It's a big wagon train due there, as you know. Anyway, we're planning to cut their trail, and if they head farther north we'll get word to Mr. Taylor and the Second—maybe even send some men. We'll be in contact with you, sir, on that."

"Right." Conway looked steadily at his adjutant. "Matt, we can't just kick Jellicoe out like that. We'd have Washington on top of us in a jiffy. I want you to catch Jellicoe with his pants down. When he makes a move, then we can hit him—but not before. You and Windy tell me he's whistled up extra help, so he's not taking any chances. You can expect anything—except if he catches you, don't expect mercy! Damn! These things always happen when we're understaffed. And with the women here, I can't give you extra men."

"I think my plan has a good chance of working, sir. Now just in case they had a line on any gossip going through Tipi Town, I've let it out that we're meeting the wagon train down by Hogshead Butte, a day's journey south of Riley's Crossing."

"You're figuring that's what they'll do—hit the train before it reaches your rendezvous? Good thinking. But why did you pick Riley's Crossing?"

"Windy suggested it, sir." Matt rose and crossed to the big wall map. "Here, sir, is Riley's Crossing. And here and here," he said, pointing, "is cover. Box elders, cottonwoods. Perfect cover for a lot of riders. Jellicoe will surely try there, figuring we're going to be at Hogshead Butte."

"He's playing a close game, Jellicoe is," Conway said. "He's planning to build Jellicoe City from supplies he gets from the plundered wagon trains. It won't cost him a cent. Meanwhile, he spreads whiskey around, making sure the local Indians get some, casting further suspicion on them for the wagon train massacres. He probably figures that eventually he'll be able to stir up enough outrage that the army will come in and wipe out the Indians for him, leaving the way clear for him to spread out even more."

There was a knock at the door, and it opened to admit First Sergeant Ben Cohen.

"First Platoon is assembled on the parade, sir."

Conway stood up.

"Sir?" Cohen began.

"Yes, Sergeant."

"Request, sir. Private Zachary has asked permission to accompany First Platoon on patrol."

"I appreciate Private Zachary's, uh, enthusiasm, Sergeant, but permission is denied."

"Yes, sir."

Conway turned to Kincaid. "And, uh, Matt?"

"Yes, sir."

"No more knife duels."

"Yes, sir."

"If I had known about that in advance, I would not have allowed it."

"I know, sir."

"And that's why I didn't know, right?"

"Uh, yes, sir."

But Conway was grinning. Then the grin vanished as he said, "Matt, you're too valuable to the army, and especially to myself and Easy Company, to risk getting gored in a knife fight. Oh, I know you impressed the Cheyenne, and it turned out to be just what was needed to cool them off. So you weren't wrong. But while you weren't wrong, you weren't right, either."

"I understand, sir." And he caught the smile in Conway's eyes as they walked out of the office.

First Platoon was lined up in two columns, the men standing by their horses.

"Lieutenant Kincaid, I don't have to tell you to be careful."

"I'll be careful, sir." Matt pulled on his gauntlets, his glance moving over to Flora Conway and her mother, who were standing in front of the commanding officer's quarters. Then he spotted Nellie and Zack on the far side of the parade. They were standing close to Corporal Wojensky's squad, which included Malone, Dobbs, Holzer, and Al Gatwin. Nellie was looking up at the flag, which was hardly moving in the windless morning, and now she turned her eyes to one of the men; Kincaid wasn't sure which one. Zachary was just staring at the dazzling spectacle of First Platoon decked out in full array.

"You'll have two scouts," Conway said as Windy Mandalian approached.

"Right, Captain. Could use another."

"I have already turned down Private Zachary's request, Windy."

"Ah, I figgered you would, Captain."

Conway turned to Kincaid. "That's about it, Lieutenant."

It was only just dawn, with the sky a raspberry color at the horizon.

"Good luck," Conway said.

"Thank you, sir," Kincaid said as he turned, giving a last pull at one of his gauntlets. "Sergeant Olsen, give the command to mount."

"Yessir!"

Olsen's command instantly filled the saddles. A horse whiffled, another shook its head, a third swept at flies with its tail. Bits clinked and jangled, leather creaked, and there was the dull thud of horses' hooves as First Platoon moved out at Olsen's order for a column of twos.

Matt Kincaid twisted around in his McClellan saddle to salute his commanding officer. As his eyes met the captain's he also saw, in his peripheral vision, the short figure behind and to the side of Conway, wearing that peaked cap over a veritable stack of wheat-colored hair; the boy now cut the air with a snappy salute.

It was over in a flash, and as they rode through the gate, Matt wished that Captain Conway had seen it.

Now the spring morning touched the dark plain, feeling its way across the prairie grass, the prints of horses and wild animals, the old ruts of wagon wheels that had already passed this way. As the light quickened, a jay called in the silver air, and a myriad of subtle colors sifted over the softening land, rousing the new day. A light wind stirred like a breath, and the goldenrod glistened near the water crossing. There were shadows there, and the soft round sound of water moving over and around the stones in the streambed.

Hidden by box elders and bullberry bushes on a rise of land, the horsebackers waited. They commanded a clear view of the crossing and its approaches, for they were high enough to see across to the other side. But they had been there an hour or more, and were beginning to grow restive.

"Might be a while," Purvis Jellicoe said. "No sense gettin' ourselves all horned up over it."

"Paw, you sure the soldiers is meetin' the train down by Hogshead Butte?"

"That's what the man here said." Purvis cut his eye to Ethan Deal, who was straddling a small dun pony.

"That's the word I heard," Deal said. "But this ain't gettin' me a horse, Jellicoe."

"Preacher, you just mind it now." Purvis's hooded eyes moved from Deal to the man at his side. "Hendry," he said softly, "a little waitin' won't hurt."

Hendry, a short, stocky man with the lobe of one of his ears missing, said, "Sure don't. Waitin' makes a man feisty. What we need for what's coming up."

Hendry had brought six men with him, his "boys." These six, as Purvis Jellicoe had instantly pointed out to his own sons, were not kin. "Man like Hendry don't usually have kin," he had explained, prior to their ally's arrival back at the north fork soddy. "Not like us—we be family." And he smiled paternally on his boys. And then, to their utter astonishment he had said, "Wish Poe was here to see all this."

Poe Jellicoe had been Poon's twin, and as such was also the youngest. But he had suddenly "up and died legal" of the croup, and there wasn't anything Purvis and his boys could do about it. But, like everything, Purvis had taken Poe's death personally, telling his sons that it was because Poe, like Poon, had been "weak and soft— just like your ma," who had died bearing him and Poon. Poe's name was mentioned so rarely that now the remaining members of the clan—Porter, Palmer, Print, Prior, and Poon—realized the gravity of the moment, that their father regarded the work to be done as no small thing, and that they'd by God better pull it off right and not make any dumb mistakes like Poon had at Jack Creek.

This, of course, included the double-cross of the Hendry bunch, which as explained by Purvis, simply meant that at the finish of the action—and the moment had to be precise so as not to be botched —when the wagon train was in the Jellicoes' hands, Hendry and his boys would also be eliminated.

The old man reached into his sagging trouser pocket now and brought out his plug of tobacco and offered some to Hendry.

"Reckon I will," the bandit said. "Always good to keep loose when there's a big action on." He grinned at Purvis Jellicoe, pleased to be working with such a professional, who was some years his senior. Then his eyes swept over the Jellicoe boys. Hendry had instructed his boys—Clay Hooligan, J. J. Bookster, Bill and Horace Wolgast, Blue Whistler, and Puck Hendrickson—that the moment the wagon train had been taken, they were to turn their artillery on the Jellicoes. "On account of seven is easier to split than thirteen," he had told them, laughing at his little joke.

Now, Hendry and Purvis smiled at each other, neither of them aware of the other's plans.

It hadn't been difficult for Windy and his two Delaware scouts to cut the trail of the Jellicoe-Hendry gang. They had followed them for several miles, the platoon keeping some distance behind them, and had finally swung wide around the outlaws as they approached Riley's Crossing.

"We can move in by that draw I showed you on the map," Windy said when he dropped back for a conference with Kincaid. "You'll get a clear view of the whole action there, and there's good cover in the cottonwoods and crackwillow."

They rode for a while in silence and then Matt said, "Too bad old Zack couldn't come along."

Windy's lined face broke into a grin. "Ain't he a corker!" But then his grin soured into a frown. "I hear they want to send him somewheres to get a doctor to look at him and to get him educated—all that. Shit, Matt, that is real dumb. That kid knows most things already. If he gets sent to school, they'll just teach all the good sense out of him."

"Didn't you ever get sent to school, Windy?"

The scout looked at him in astonishment at such an outrageous thought. "You bet your ass I didn't. I knew everything I needed by the time I was Zack's age—ten or thereabouts." He wagged his head at the end of his long neck. "Shit, they send that boy to school, he'll be dead of dumbness by the time he's twenty."

"I believe it's Mrs. Dodgson's idea," Matt said.

Windy spat, then said sourly, "Figgers."

They were soon positioned in the cottonwoods and crackwillow, looking down across a wide meadow that bordered Riley's Crossing.

"They'll be over in them box elders by now," Windy said as he took Matt's glasses and focused on the trees on the far side of the meadow. "Yup. I just seen somethin' move. Probably Jellicoe's jaws."

"Got any idea when the wagons will get here?"

"Couple of hours. See, we figured if we'd went down

to meet 'em at Hogshead Butte, it'd be sometime toward nightfall. We're a good distance north of Hogshead."

Matt pulled out his watch and snapped open the lid. Closing it, he looked at the men around him. "Sergeant Olsen?"

"Yes, sir."

"I expect the wagon train shortly, although it could take longer, even a lot longer."

"Yes, sir."

"You'll be in charge here. Windy and I will be riding to the other side of that cutbank, across the river to intercept the wagons. If we don't get back, you already have your orders."

"Yes, sir."

As they rode away from the platoon, Windy said, "Well, old son, I hope you can sell the master of that wagon train on your crazy, crazy plan."

"So do I." He twisted in his saddle to look closely at the scout. "Do you think it's crazy?"

"I sure do. But it's the only plan I've heard in this good while I been a scout that has got some real sense to it." He grinned and waved his hand at a fly that had landed on his nose. "You know, this Indian fighting can get awful boring unless you put some powder into it now and again."

"There she be, boys."

The wagon train had rounded the cutbank, and now the lead horses were just at the river crossing. But the men watching from the box elders could only see the white tops of the wagons, for the crossing was dense with cottonwood.

"See any soldiers?" Poon asked.

"Nary a one," Purvis answered.

"There ain't any," Hendry said, taking off his Stetson

hat and putting it on again, then checking his holstered sixguns, his Winchester, and finally his fly, which had a rip in it, though minor.

"You wasn't expecting soldiers, was you, Poon?" Porter asked slyly.

"Nope. But you never can tell. Paw's always said to be ready for anything."

"They're sure moving slow."

Across the meadow, the men of the First Platoon had also noted the slowness of the wagon train.

"They're all slow," Stretch Dobbs observed, "but this one appears slower than ever."

"Maybe they got a broken wheel or something," Al Gatwin said.

"Or could be a lame horse or two," Reb McBride suggested.

"Can't see the emigrants," Malone said. "Those leaves are thicker than bedbugs."

In the stand of box elders, Old Man Jellicoe had his eyes stuck to the field glasses. "There they be," he said again. "Ready the boys now."

But it wasn't until the lead wagon had finally crossed the shallow water and the team of horses was pulling up the slight rise into the meadow that a gasp went up from Purvis Jellicoe.

"For Chissake!" The old man was gripping the glasses until his knuckles were white.

"The Injuns beat us to it!" Hendry said, his grainy voice tight with anger and alarm.

They gaped at the scene below as the wagon train pulled farther into the meadow, with Indians on the drivers' seats, and others escorting the caravan on horses along each side.

"Calm yourself," Old Man Jellicoe said with a chuckle.

"Don't bust a gallus there, Hendry." He chuckled again. "By God, who would've guessed that those kind boys would do our hard work for us already." And he lowered the glasses, his whole face wrapped in a big grin. "They've already took the wagon train, an' we'll just get on down there an' rescue her!"

"They're actin' funny, Jellicoe." Hendry's voice terminated the astonished silence that gripped them after Purvis spoke.

"They're like drunk," Prior said. "Look at that one ridin' his horse backwards and pretendin' to shoot arrers into hisself!"

"They are plumb crazy," said the old man. "Or more'n likely they got into some liquor. Boys, this one's going to be the easiest pickin's of all!"

"Right now, Paw!"

"You hold it! We want 'em just right. We'll let 'em feel the meadow a bit longer, let 'em feel nice and soft and safe—the fuckers."

On the other side of the meadow, Windy Mandalian wore a big grin on his face. "By golly, I do believe you did it, Matt. It's working."

Malone, Dobbs, and the other men stared in fascination at the antics of the Indians in the meadow. Even though they had been instructed by Kincaid and Windy Mandalian as to what to expect, it was a shocking surprise to them all.

The wagons were strung out across almost the entire length of the meadow now, and the Indians rode up and down the train's length, sitting backwards on their horses, with their tunics on back to front, their hair flying, some doing handstands on their ponies, others climbing under their horses' necks, wrapping their legs up around the animals' withers. Others ran crouched underneath some of the horses, giving the impression that they were the horses being ridden by the animals. Still others shot arrows at one another—but arrows made from bent branches, which flew from slack bowstrings and went nowhere.

"That's them goddamn Contrastings or whatever they're called," said Ethan Deal, but nobody heard him as they rode slowly down into the meadow, laughing at the Contraries' antics, sitting loose and easy in their saddles.

"They're sitting game," Prior Jellicoe said. "They only got some kids' bows and arrows."

He said this as one of the riders somehow shot an arrow at himself and fell, laughing, off his horse.

"Drunker'n a barrel of pickled fish," Purvis said, pulling his Spencer out of its saddle boot. "We can catch up on our target practice, boys." He was watching three of the Indians who were making their horses walk backwards.

"I'll take that one on the right," Hendry said at his side.

"An' while you're doin' that," laughed Purvis, "I'll bag me them two on the left."

He had hardly said those words when an eagle-bone whistle pierced the air. The three Indians who had been moving their horses backwards suddenly kicked them forward, causing Purvis and Hendry to miss their targets.

Now the Jellicoes and Hendry's boys all opened fire at once. But the Indians suddenly turned their horses and raced back to the crossing.

At the same moment, all the wagon teams were whipped into a gallop, and the wagons were quickly brought into an L formation, with the attacking outlaws riding into the inside of the L.

This was when the outlaws first noticed—entirely too late—that the sides of the wagons, where the canvas tops met the wooden sides, were bristling with rifle bar-

172

rels. The emigrants, safely concealed within the wagons, opened fire all at once, and the outlaws were caught in a merciless crossfire. They didn't have any more chance than they'd given the wagon train at Jack Creek.

Reb McBride's bugle sounded and First Platoon, led by Matt Kincaid, galloped down to cut off any retreat. In minutes it was over. Hendry had been wounded mortally, and lay dying, facedown in a clump of sage. All his men were dead or wounded; only one remained ambulatory, and held his hands high above his head as the soldiers arrived. Of the Jellicoes, Porter, Poon, and Print were all down with wounds. Prior and Palmer had thrown down their guns and had their hands stretched high above their heads.

But now, suddenly, a special drama took everyone's attention as, unnoticed during the battle, Ethan Deal had taken the opportunity to commandeer the horse he was riding, and now was galloping toward the river crossing and the relative safety of the cottonwoods. Behind him raced Purvis Jellicoe on his big dappled gray stud horse. The old man's rage came screaming across the meadow. "You sonofabitch! You sold us out!"

Suddenly Deal's little dun horse, who was losing ground to the big dappled gray, stumbled and threw its rider. But Deal wasn't finished. He rose to his knees, still gripping the old muzzle-loader, which he claimed to have picked up back in Nebraska and with which he'd shot Running Bull and Jessie the mule.

But Jellicoe's big horse was right on top of him, and Purvis, rising in his stirrups, shrieking curses, fired his Spencer with one hand. The bullet caught Ethan Deal in the chest, knocking him flat on his back.

"He's a goner," soneone said, as Purvis, racing by, fired another round into the body of Ethan Deal.

But almost before the words had lost their echo, Deal rose up and, with that old rifle, shot Purvis Jellicoe—

Old Man Jellicoe, who had ridden with Quantrill and Bloody Bill Anderson—right through the back of his head.

When Windy and Matt and some of the platoon reached him, Deal was lying on his back, with the blood dark on his torn shirt, his ragged broadcloth coat.

"By God, preacher, that was shootin'," Windy said.

"Told you, mister scout, I could shoot the eyelash off a rabbit, by God."

And Ethan Deal closed his eyes and died.

Windy suddenly stopped chewing. "By golly," he said, "That man has still got his hat on."

seventeen _____

The regimental ambulance, with its team of horses, waited outside the orderly room. Beyond, at the center of the parade, Easy Company stood in formation, at ease.

As the door of the orderly room opened and Captain Conway, accompanied by his wife and mother-in-law, appeared, Lieutenant Matt Kincaid called the company to attention.

"Have the men stand at ease, Lieutenant," Conway said. And as Matt gave the order, the captain turned back to his two ladies.

"Sergeant Olsen and an escort will accompany you to Regiment, Mavis," Conway said.

"That's thoughtful of you, Warner dear."

"Regulations, ma'am," said Conway, with a teasing smile.

Suddenly Mrs. Dodgson stepped forward and embraced him, to his embarrassment and to the amusement of Flora. Then she released her son-in-law and spun on

Matt Kincaid, who had moved into the small circle to offer his goodbye.

"Ah, Lieutenant!" And she enveloped Matt in a hug, to the great amusement of both Conways.

Releasing Kincaid, she stepped back, her eyes darting to the entire company standing there on the parade.

"Warner, what a delightful send-off."

"Mavis, it's morning muster. But the men are delighted to wish you their best for your trip."

"Of course, dear. Now I want to say something about that young boy. I really am put out that you will not permit me to take him with me."

"Mavis, we've been over all that. Regiment is still looking for his parents."

"Warner, I find that difficult to believe. How can they take so long? How can they be so heartless?"

"Mother, please—let's not go into it now. Warner and Matt have to take morning muster."

"And the girl, Nellie. Ah, there you are, dear," she beamed as Nellie appeared from behind Matt Kincaid. "Dear, I did think badly of you at one time, but I offer you my apologies. And my congratulations. I understand that you and—somebody—are getting married."

Nellie had turned crimson. It was Matt Kincaid who rescued her. "It's not definite yet, Mrs. Dodgson, but Private Gatwin has asked permission of the captain to marry Nellie."

"That's just what I said, Lieutenant."

"Goodbye, Mrs. Dodgson." Nellie's smile was soft and—so it seemed to Matt—wistful.

Mavis Dodgson turned. "Well, I suppose I can't disturb the men in their ranks. But there are some I wish to say goodbye to. I'd thought there would be time. Oh, dear." She stood looking out at the assembled company, her fingers touching her cheek. "But I do wish you'd give a special goodbye to Sergeant Maloney and Sergeant

176

Ruthouse, and that nice officer, Cohen. Flora, dear, will you do that?"

"Of course, Mother. Now why don't you get into the ambulance, so that they can get started. It's a long drive."

"All three of them promised to write me, you know. And I'll be sending recipes to Sergeant Ruthouse."

Conway's eyes closed for a moment.

As her daughter urged her toward the waiting vehicle, Mrs. Dodgson spied the short figure standing with his hands stiffly at his sides.

"Ah, now there we are. Zachary. Zachary, do come and say goodbye to me."

Zachary remained motionless.

At that point Ben Cohen, who had been holding the company, walked over and saluted the captain and said, "Sir, while the company is at ease, may the first sergeant have permission to say goodbye to Mrs. Dodgson?"

"Permission granted, Sergeant Cohen."

"Oh, what a lovely way to say it, Sergeant." And her hand flew out to Ben Cohen, who took it as though it were a piece of cake with very brittle icing. "Goodbye, dear Sergeant."

"Goodbye, Mrs. Dodgson."

"But I want to say goodbye to Zachary."

Ben Cohen, relieved to escape the social vice in which he'd suddenly found himself, stepped back.

"Private Zachary," he snapped. "Front and center."

Zack, wearing a cut-down uniform and campaign hat, stepped forward to face the first sergeant.

"You may say goodbye to Mrs. Dodgson, Private."

Zack's eyes flew in desperation to Windy, who was grinning at him.

"Go ahead, Zack," the scout said. Turning to Cohen, he muttered, "Understand you got him on the roster."

"Good way to hide him."

"The captain and Kincaid know that?"

"It was their idea."

"I'm proud of that kind of thinking," Windy said.

Mrs. Dodgson had started toward Zachary, but stopped. Turning to Conway, she said, "Warner, can't you see the boy needs a woman's love and care?"

"He has Nellie and Flora."

"Nellie—I cannot believe she's to be married! Things happen so quickly. But if the poor boy could only speak! I've often wondered what he would say if he spoke, if he could just say something." She turned to the boy, who was standing at attention.

"Zachary, let me ask you just once more—wouldn't you like to come back East with me and live in a nice big house with hot water and clean sheets and everything, and have friends your own age to play with, and go to a nice school?"

Her smile was radiant as she bent her head to one side and opened her arms to welcome him.

Zachary said nothing. He was still standing at attention.

"Private Zachary," said Ben Cohen. "You may be at ease and answer Mrs. Dodgson."

The boy stood at ease now, his corn-yellow hair almost in his eyes.

"Oh, you do need a haircut! Wouldn't you like that, dear boy? A nice haircut?"

The boys hands were at his sides, and now he started to raise them while Windy watched, ready to interpret any sign he might use.

But Zachary dropped his hands. And standing not at all rigid, but firmly inside himself; he looked straight at Mavis Dodgson and said, "No. I don't want a haircut, ma'am."

Warner Conway felt the grin starting up behind his face, but managed to control it.

"He spoke! He said something!" Mavis Dodgson spun around to look at each of them. "Isn't that marvelous! He can speak!"

When she turned back to Zachary, Conway felt his heart sink. He was about to say something, to insist that she get into the ambulance because the men were waiting to get through morning muster, because, this nonsense had gone on all too long, when suddenly, and totally unexpectedly, he saw for the very first time the true caliber of his mother-in-law.

Mavis Dodgson seemed smaller as she took two steps forward, until she was standing very close to the boy. And then she reached out her hand and touched the sleeve of his cut-down uniform. Just the sleeve. That was all. She didn't say a word, but turned quickly, not looking at anyone, and walked toward the ambulance and got in. And in only a few minutes she was gone.

That night at dinner, Flora Conway said, "I find it so incredible that the Indians would do what they did, Warner. I mean, to help the army. To risk being shot and killed."

"I find it rather incredible myself," Conway said, looking over at their two dinner guests. "What do you and Windy have to say about that, Matt?"

"I can tell you, sir, I am mighty relieved it worked as well as it did. We're rid of the Jellicoes and we've built a solid friendship with Faraway Eagle." He looked across at Windy, who nodded.

"But I still don't see how you got them to do it," said Flora. "I mean, if it's a military secret, then I don't want to know. But it seems so unbelievable, that strange behavior and all. Did you tell them to do all that backwards business to fool the Jellicoes and put them off guard?"

Matt grinned. "I simply told them the situation and

179

asked them to drive the wagon train with the emigrants. We didn't want to risk a confrontation on Jellicoe's terms, so we had to draw him out."

"A tricky moment," Conway said. "Because you couldn't be sure how they'd play it."

"All we could be sure of," said Windy, "was that they'd be contrary." He grinned at Matt. "And that they were."

Watch for

EASY COMPANY AND THE BIG GAME HUNTER

twenty-eighth novel in the exciting
EASY COMPANY series

Coming in May!

EASY COMPANY

MORE ROUGH RIDING ACTION FROM JOHN WESLEY HOWARD